Christmas
In Pilaf

Apple Pie

D1529055

André Bernier

Merry Christmas! 2017

Blessings! André Bernier

Christmas In Pilaf - Apple Pie.
Copyright © 2015 by André Bernier.
All rights reserved.

The author can be contacted by email at
pilafpublishing@yahoo.com, or on Facebook by
liking the "André Bernier Fan Page."

Dedicated to Pastor J. Michael Bragg,
one of my cherished and trusted spiritual mentors.

Iron sharpeneth iron;
so a man sharpeneth
the countenance of his friend.

Proverbs 27:17
(KJV)

Prologue

When I took up my pen and paper in the summer of 2014 to start outlining a different kind of Christmas novel, and as it came together, there was a little voice inside of me saying that this might become a fun Christmas tradition. That's how the first holiday novel, _Christmas In Pilaf: The Journal_, was born. After five months of writing, proofing, and reproofing during every spare minute of my time, I dismissed the idea of a sequel and simply enjoyed the dividends of hearing from people who really enjoyed last year's visit to Pilaf.

This spring, people were starting to ask me if there was a sequel in the works. After a pleasant rest from writing, I started entertaining the idea. At first, I thought about writing a traditional, third-person style novel. Before making that decision, I used social media to ask whether you wanted another journal-style book from Danny Rice's perspective, or a traditional novel. Much to my surprise, the result was unanimous! Everyone wanted more from Danny Rice's journal.

If you have not yet read the first book from last year, I highly recommend it before you begin this year's journey. While you certainly could read this one without book one under your belt, you'll miss many of the fun references to certain things that happened last year in Pilaf.

Also, as I recommended in book one, read each day's morning and evening journal entry aloud with your family on the matching day. Have fun with trying to figure out where the plot of the story is going. I guarantee you there will be plenty of surprises along the way, and lots of great stories to bolster your faith during this most Holy time we call Christmas.

Apple Pie

"Statistics are to baseball what a flaky
crust is to apple pie."

Harry Reasoner
Founder of CBS's 60 Minutes

Sunday, November 22, 2015, 6:45 a.m.

Harry Buser has me thinking about certain things far too deeply these days, mainly what we perceive as reality. He has been visiting the store quite a bit lately, usually to meet Uncle Ben for coffee at least twice a week ever since the last of the leaves fell off the tree just outside Bailey's. I've tried not to disturb them as it looked like their conversation was deep and intentional. Uncle Ben had his Bible open on a few of those occasions, although I'm not sure how much of it is all related.

So here I am, sitting at my peaceful kitchen table, watching the coils of steam coming up from my cup of coffee as I marvel at the pattern. The occasional corkscrews of steam, as fleeting as they are, look so beautiful that I can't help to wonder how something like that can be random and chaotic. Neither word seems to be an appropriate label for something that can be so spellbinding. There are simply too few of these quiet moments for me. As much as I enjoy technology, I must find a way to break the suction with my so-called smartphone and tablet. There are far too many nights when I get drawn into a virtual world of tweets, posts, and games between friends after everyone has beat me to the first set of nighttime dreams. After I realize how much time has passed by, I'm often disappointed when I feel as though I lost that time to a thief on the other side of a casino table. I don't gamble, and I never will, but I have to imagine that it describes how I feel at that moment. Even here in the cozy, deliberately-paced town of Pilaf, technology lurks. But not at this moment. My phone is off (not that it would ring at 6:45 a.m.). My tablet is off. My Bible is open to Proverbs Chapter 17. So much wisdom jam-packed into that one chapter.

Jennifer, Joel, and Jessie are just beginning to stir. Sammy looks like he is dreaming. He is on the kitchen chair beside me with his eyes closed. I saw his whiskers and one of his paws gently twitch. I wonder what he is dreaming about? Does Sammy ever dream about any of us? I like to think so, but only God knows.

Sunday, November 22, 2015, 8:07 p.m.

It has been a very warm autumn that keeps on giving. Today was no exception. It seems odd to feel warm, dry breezes when the trees are bare and the sweet scent of fallen leaves is filling the air. Even stranger was seeing some of the church sanctuary windows open during today's worship service. When will the other shoe drop? And when it does, will it be a size you might find on Hulk Hogan? The later it gets without experiencing our first cold snap, the more suspect I become. Stormy Windham seems to think this may continue for just a little while longer, perhaps even through Thanksgiving. Last year's cold rain and wet snow went right through everyone who went to the annual Thanksgiving Day high school football game. Perhaps the atmosphere is trying to make up for last year.

It was also odd seeing everyone at church this morning wearing something you might find in late September or October from light jackets, pastel colors, and even a few brave souls donning short-sleeved polo shirts. Uncle Ben and George the mailman seemed to spend a long time discussing something between two pews, while everyone else headed out to enjoy the warm breezes and unusually bright November sunshine. I was in the latter group since their conversation seemed nowhere near wrapping up.

One of the advantages of a long, warm, and dry autumn has been the near constant scent of autumn leaves. I love that. It doesn't take much motion of my feet along the thick carpet of leaves to enhance the familiar autumn scent. It's a comforting aroma, much like the scent of turkey dinner on Thanksgiving Day, or taking in the rustic fragrance of Bailey's Country Store. By and large we take the wonderful gift of smell so much for granted until one thinks deeply about this ability. Scents, which are powerful memory-recall vehicles, can act like a warning sign, enhance the sense of taste, and promote the sense of well-being. Who doesn't like the scent of lilacs in the spring, or their wife or girlfriend's favorite perfume? Who hasn't benefitted from the early warning sign that something is burning in the kitchen? Yet, how often do people take that wonderful sense for absolute granted? I try not to, especially when a scent catches my attention, good or bad. Naturally, I prefer the good ones.

We grilled burgers out on the deck tonight. There hasn't been any snow to speak of this autumn and the grill has had more use than normal much to the delight of Joel and Jessie. I must admit that being surrounded by the aroma of the smoky blue haze from burgers on the grill does something to the soul, even if the sun was well below the horizon.

Monday, November 23, 2015, 9:05 a.m.

I was surprised to see Miss Miller in the store this morning before the school day started. She eyed the apples, picked a few of them up for a closer examination, then came to the counter with a small container of cranberry juice. She asked if I expected any Melrose apples in my supply, and if I expected that the Cortland apples would still be around in a few weeks. Ah, yes. Of course! It's almost time for Miss Miller's famous apple pie. She has never shopped here for her apples in the past. According to my sources, she typically runs out to Buckley's Fruit Farm for enough apples to bake a half-dozen pies just after Thanksgiving. With all I've heard about Miss Miller's pies, I've never had the privilege of sampling them. It's a bucket list item for sure, especially now that I have actually sampled one of Mrs. Krumm's sugar cookies as of last year. There are few Pilaf items that remain on my list of things to try. Perhaps this year I'll score a slice if Miss Miller comes back for what she needs.

Joel and Jessie are in pre-Holiday mode once more, but they seem less focused on the lack of sensibility of a short school week. In fact, they seem to be less fidgety as well. Could it be the unseasonable warmth that is the root, or perhaps a bit of maturity as they are a year older? It does not seem as though they are scrambling to complete assignments like last year. Perhaps that's it. A part of me misses the Thanksgiving and Christmas mayhem. I must be careful, though. That's something I should not be caught admitting to them as a part of me is enjoying the more thoughtful conversation at the breakfast-table.

Uncle Ben stopped by for coffee earlier this morning. There was only a minor chill in the store, just enough to accentuate the coffee's flavor. I have not used the wood stove yet to supplement the store's heat this autumn. If I did, the unusual warmth of the November sun would have made the store uncomfortably warm by noon. The sun is shining once more today and the thermometer on the store's porch is proudly touting 59°F. Without much rain in the last few weeks, the roads are getting a bit dusty. It's odd since the dust is equally spread out onto the carpet of fallen leaves. Whenever I've been out to kick around the leaves with Joel and Jessie, I've kicked up quite a bit of dust as well. You can see it especially when the sun is low and about to set.

Monday, November 23, 2015, 5:17 p.m.

There has been a steady increase in business over the past few Mondays. That's a fairly common trend in the month of November since Pilafians are getting ready for Thanksgiving. By the time Thanksgiving eve arrives, things get very quiet in the store. Last year, I closed the store at 4 o'clock that day. No one came in after 3 o'clock. I could hear the little nuance sounds of the store that are ordinarily masked by the day's busyness. It reminded me of the need to create time and space so that I could hear that still small voice that Elijah heard in 1 Kings 19. My conversation with Him that afternoon was so natural and peaceful as I let myself feel the joy of the Lord's presence. Time was irrelevant in that hour for a reason that I cannot explain using words. I'm prayerfully expecting the same in a few days as Pilaf gets busy with pre-Thanksgiving plans. I'll officially lock the doors at 4 o'clock, but I suspect that the store will be quiet for an hour or more leading up to that time.

George stopped by during his afternoon mail route today. He is always smiling, but it takes on an unspeakable dimension, a kind of gleam during Thanksgiving week. I asked him the usual questions, namely, if his Bing Crosby Christmas CD was in ready-reach, if his neatly boxed Christmas decorations were out of his attic, and what new decoration he was planning for Pilaf this year. The answers were predictable: "Yes, yes, and I'm not telling you."

That last answer was delivered with such a wonderful "Fred Rogers" tone that I could not help letting out a chuckle. Of course, George was never going to let the Christmas cat out of the bag. Every year, I muse about how I might get him to inadvertently spill the beans, but it always ends up as an exercise in futility. Despite his reluctance to share even the slightest details or smallest hints, I truly believe that George would be disappointed if I ever stopped probing for the answer. He did tell me that he would be staying in town this year, so his decorations are not up yet unlike this time last year. Naturally, like everyone in Pilaf, I'm wondering what he has up his sleeve for this year's Christmas display. Do I dare attempt to sneak a peek again like last year? If I do, I'm thinking of convincing Officer Caputo to help me so that he can't surprise me with his whirly lights and attract attention. How is it that he always seems to show up at some of the most inopportune moments? On second thought, I think steering clear might be the best way to go.

Our Pilaf Warriors have struggled some this year. Last year's star players were mostly seniors. This year, we have a lot of new talent, but the sophomores and even a few starting freshmen have been no match for some of our area teams now sporting talented seniors. The Thanksgiving day game against the Borger Bulldogs will mean either a break-even year or a losing year. Our current standing is 4-5.

Stormy Windham talked about our current warm and dry pattern coming to a "soft end" toward Thanksgiving. I hope we can hang onto this until after the game on Thanksgiving morning.

Tuesday, November 24, 2015, 10:04 a.m.

Sammy has provided Bailey's customers with unexpected, furry greetings this morning. For only the second time in Sammy's life, he came with me to the store. It was out of necessity. Not that Sammy can't guard the house for an extended stretch of time. We have left him to "guard the house" in the past during quick, overnight family trips with a cat food dispenser to be sure that his meals were available. That was certainly not the concern this time. It was Jennifer's pre-Thanksgiving meat pies that needed a slow cool-down from the oven this morning. Neither of us could be there to "pie sit." The vestibule has been too warm in this weather pattern to sequester the pies there, away from Sammy's feline temptation. Jennifer did not want to miss her weekly women's Bible study, so I put Sammy in his carrier and off we went to the store.

Sammy was unsure where we were going. Most of the time, the crate means a visit to the vet. He let me know that he was not happy. Oh, how I wish I could speak "cat" to let him know that he would love his destination. Reassuring and gentle words only served to distract him from thinking that a vet was waiting to see him until he saw the front of Bailey's. Suddenly, his countenance changed and the world was rosy.

It had been some time since he was last here, but he clearly remembered what seemed to be his favorite spot to watch life go by. I could not have picked a better place myself. It's the little bay window to the right of the store's front door that Joel and Drake decorated with blue LED Christmas lights last year. The space was made for Sammy.

He spent most of the morning bird-watching from his post, but he always hopped down from the window to greet everyone who came in. Most cats I know run and hide with every new person coming into the picture. Not Sammy. This has to be the most social cat I have ever known. He seems to take great pleasure in harnessing his natural curiosity by introducing himself to everyone who came into the store, whether they came in to sit and chat with a cup of coffee, or to grab a few items on the run. He seems to take quite the liking to Uncle Ben. We've seen this dynamic at our house, so it was no surprise when Sammy jumped up on a small stand beside him. It was clearly an invitation to be petted and scratched under the chin.

Uncle Ben met Harry Buser here once more today. They were discussing something with such focus that, had there been an earthquake or nearby explosion, I don't think they would have noticed. Must be heavy stuff.

Tuesday, November 24, 2015, 8:32 p.m.

Sammy has been sleeping much of the evening. I brought him home after the lunch crowd thinned. Jennifer said that Sammy's visit to Bailey's must have energized him so much that he spent the afternoon jumping up from one window to the next like a crazy cat. Perhaps he was looking for a spot like the little bay window at the store. We have none at our house. He was so busy trying to convince us that we needed a bay window at the house, that he was in a deep sleep on our bed by the time I came home from the store. He is still there now. He hasn't moved so much as a whisker for the last few hours, unusual since he is usually asking for his dinner by now. I think I'll need to wake him by opening a can of his food after finishing this post. Nothing brings him out of a sleep faster than the sound of a cat food can being opened.

Jennifer and I are so fortunate to have two children that are always naturally joyful, but their level of joy jumped up today after school. Neither of them brought home any homework. Tomorrow's half-day at school serves little purpose beyond acting as an exercise in seeing how well the teachers can contain the kids' enthusiasm. The teachers do themselves no favor by letting them eat more sugar cookies than they ever would at home. Yet, all of these moments in time are as special for Joel and Jessie as they were for us when we were their age. I can't remember any specifics of what happened on the day before Thanksgiving when I was in 5th or 8th grade, but with great clarity I can recall the adrenalin rush of walking home from school with my Thanksgiving artwork. I knew it was sure to find a home on the refrigerator or taped to one of our windows. That artwork has become much more sophisticated nowadays, but whatever comes home with them tomorrow will get the same treatment as my artwork did many decades ago.

Mr. Rayburn stopped in before I closed the store today. He's been doing that a little more since the summer recess. He picked up a few items and we chatted a little about the nuances of this year's group of kids. Among his items were two apples. I saw him taking a close look at some of the varieties I had. He had two Jazz apples. These are great eating apples but I've never had them in a pie and wondered how they would taste. I almost brought up Miss Miller's famous apple pies, but I did not want to seem like I was meddling. Still, as often as both have been in here, I have yet to see them in Bailey's together at the same time. I can picture every other combination of people over the span that I've been back in Pilaf, now almost two years, but never Mr. Rayburn and Miss Miller. Hmmmm.

Wednesday, November 25, 2015, 9:20 a.m.

We had a crazy breakfast run this morning, much more than usual. I had to make several pots of coffee between 6 a.m. and 8 a.m. At the end of it all, my pastry counter looked oddly barren, peppered with scone and Danish crumbs around two remaining doughnuts, one powdered, and one plain. That was twenty minutes ago. Having had only a small cup of oatmeal before leaving the house earlier today, I saw to it that only one doughnut remained. My face gave away which one remains in the case. It's a great feeling to realize that we had just enough for the day. That doesn't happen too often.

Donald Buckley came in for a late morning visit today. He's usually so busy at the orchard and pressing barn that I typically don't see him that often between apple harvest time and New Year's Day. He said this year's crop was so abundant that he wondered if I'd like a few more apples and jugs of fresh cider for the Holidays. With a few more people coming in this year asking about different apple varieties, I took him up on the offer. Donald gave me a great deal. The price on apple products this year will surely put a smile on all of our Pilaf pie-makers, whether it's here or at Giammalvo's Market. I'll have to tell Mr. Rayburn to let Miss Miller know that I will carry more than usual this year.

Remembering the play time that Jim and I had in Mr. Buckley's orchard has always been a great memory. As kids, we had our favorite rendezvous trees. They were not something we revered for their crop, but for their ability to provide the perfect lookout perches and hiding places. Mr. Buckley never had to worry about us sampling his fruit. Jim and I both had not yet developed a taste for apples. Be that as it may, I would hate to admit to Mr. Buckley what we occasionally would do with a few of those apples when we felt like a friendly challenge of strength. We would mark an apple and hurl it as far as we could to see which one of us could throw it the farthest. Jim invariably won every contest of that sort. He loved playing baseball in the school yard.

As a kid, I always thought that being an orchard owner did not require a lot of work. The trees did all the work, right? All that changed when, as a young teenager, I walked in on an episode of Mr.Rogers' Neighborhood where Mr. McFeely, the delivery man, brought Mr. Rogers a videocassette recording about how apple juice is made and bottled. It was not only fascinating, it made me realize how wrong I was about the work involved in the apple business. Not only did I have a brand new appreciation of what Donald Buckley did for a living, but I dared to sample apple juice and apple cider with a new perspective. Suddenly, I liked apple juice! It seemed to happen overnight. To this day, there is nothing better in the autumn than a cup of hot, spiced apple cider. What in the world was I thinking when I turned my nose up at warmed apple cider? Even Joel and Jessie like warmed and spiced apple cider. Granted, it usually comes with a sugar cookie or pastry. Perhaps that was the key ingredient that I had been missing.

Wednesday, November 25, 2015, 4:22 p.m.

All the talk of apples and cider made me think of nothing else all day. Thirty minutes before closing the store, I broke out one of the two quarts of Buckley's apple cider and warmed it with a stick of cinnamon bark. Just like last year, Bailey's was quiet after both Uncle Ben and Harry Buser left. That was an hour ago. I'm convinced that everyone needs at least a small nook that can act as their place of solitude. Mine is now larger than a small nook. I relish the smallest sounds that I can hear during those moments of quiet. I can hear the slightest breeze, the low hum of the cooler, and even small ticks of the foundation as it expands and contracts with the changing of the season. One of the dearest sounds to me is when one of the store shutters occasionally gets caught in a wind eddy. The low frequency bounce is something that even I might miss and filter out as background noise unless I pay close attention. All these sounds are comfort sounds that require the act of listening intently. It's similar to hearing that still, small voice of God. Our heavenly Father isn't going to come crashing in and demand your attention, although He certainly could. Instead, He chooses to whisper to us. It's up to us to want to quiet ourselves enough to hear His sweet voice.

It's cloudy and mild, 57°F, and the wind is picking up a little. It has been a very warm fall thus far, but the breezes that I can actually hear through the trees are winds of change according to Stormy. The season's first polar push is aiming for us, but according to Stormy, it comes without the drama of a significant snowfall. I take no issue with that, although it certainly would have been fun sitting in the football bleachers tomorrow watching our Warriors trying to move the pigskin on a snow-covered field.

It has been almost ten years since we've experienced a significant snowfall on Thanksgiving. They are easy to recall since a heavy snowfall on Thanksgiving Day is not all that common. It's fascinating how I can remember all of them with great detail, yet I have trouble remembering what we did only a couple of years ago. My earliest recollection of a snowy Thanksgiving was when I was eight years old. Mom and Dad were both in a happy place planning for the guests we were expecting for Thanksgiving dinner. I can actually pull the specific aromas of the feast blended with our home's unique fragrance from my memory and seemingly smell it again in my mind. Extra tables and chairs were set up in every imaginable place. I don't remember anyone complaining about how horrible the roads were as our relatives arrived. It didn't seem to bother anyone, perhaps because there were so few people on the roads. I remember watching Barry Burbank talking about the snowstorm during the noon newscast while looking out the window right next to our television. The snowflakes were mammoth. Seeing across the street was a chore as the snow was falling heavily. The scene made the coziness of that Thanksgiving an indelible memory. On a day like today, it gives me pause to smile when I'm enjoying the ambience of a completely quiet store.

I'm on my second cup of apple cider. I locked the front door some thirty minutes ago. All of my work is done here. I could have left much sooner, but these moments of solitude are sweet. The family chaos of two young kids running around the house with holiday excitement are equally as sweet, but in a different way. I appreciate both. I'll bring home the remainder of the cider so we can enjoy it together as a family tonight and tomorrow.

Thanksgiving Day,
November 26, 2015, 6:52 a.m.

Jennifer had been up for a little while when I wandered into the kitchen. You can tell that it's Thanksgiving. She is dancing around with a joyful, schoolgirl spring in her step as she tweaks this, opens that, and checks all the other things that have become a culinary work-in-progress. Even before seeing this delightful scene, my nose told me that it was Thanksgiving morning. Jennifer knows that cooking maple-glazed bacon stirs me from my slumber. How can you wake up grumpy while smelling something so heavenly? I'm not the only one. Sammy has been pacing the kitchen floor, schmoozing both of us with head and body rubs trying to convince us to toss him a scrap.

I did briefly wake much earlier in the wee hours this morning. I was hoping to see a triple digit but saw 2:44 a.m. instead. I've not had a triple for a while. I'm due. The full moon was casting its silvery-blue light on Pilaf. It would have been very difficult to ignore. I checked in with Joel and Jessie. Both were sound asleep. I will never grow weary of watching them sleep. I often smile thinking that God watches me sleep. His love for us is unquantifiable.

The love we have for our children simply pales in comparison to God's love for us. While it's a comfort to know this through His Word, it's also something impossible to completely grasp this side of eternity. I kissed each of them before heading back to my own pillow and wondered how I would handle the day when I would no longer have the luxury of peeking in on our children, far away in a college dorm, or as they venture out to the place that God has called them to be.

Jessie's papier mâché turkey that she brought home from school yesterday found a home in the middle of our breakfast counter this morning. I'm glad that Jennifer briefed me on what it was. I must have had a strange look on my face when I first saw it there. Initially, it looked like a giant, mangled wad of tissue. I knew that Jennifer would not have left it there unless it had some significance. Even after she told me what it was, my mind worked hard to see it. I'll know now to make a big fuss over the avant garde sculpture when Jessie comes in for breakfast.

It's a lot colder this morning, just like Stormy predicted. While the ground is largely bare, there seems to be a kiss of something frozen in small patches on the grass. I confirmed it when I looked out on the deck and flicked the light on. I don't even think you could call it a dusting, but the cold front that slid by must have tried to leave a subtle calling card before moving on, letting the full moon flood the landscape again. It's 26°F. Looks like we'll need to adjust our attire compared to the last few weeks of mild air and sunshine, especially for our annual trek out to the football stadium. Borger is only fifteen minutes away, but we will leave in plenty of time to position ourselves close to the fifty-yard line on the away bench. This year, we are all heading to the game since we are doing something unique for Thanksgiving that doesn't require Jennifer to stay behind. She wanted to be a part of the football fun this year and came up with a way to do that. Innovation is my beautiful bride's middle name.

Thanksgiving Day,
November 26, 2015, 8:22 p.m.

What a memorable day on so many levels. The most distinct element of the day was the joy, so tangible, yet so supernatural. It seemed to ooze into dimensions well beyond our five senses, with a sense of supernatural joy returning from a place far above our realm. These are things which are spiritually discerned. The apostle Paul was all too familiar with this when he wrote about things of this nature in 1 Corinthians 2:13-14. It makes me sad to think that there are too many people in the world to whom none of this makes any sense. That's why we are to be the salt and light of the Earth, to make the things of God attractive to those who do not know Him.

Jennifer was ready for the annual Thanksgiving Day high school football game before anyone else. She never seemed to be overly interested in years past, but after she saw the glow in our eyes as Joel, Jessie, and I arrived home from last year's exciting game, my guess is that she wanted to be a part of that memory, not only for herself, but for Joel and Jessie, too. At least this year, we weren't going to have to deal with heavy rain and snow, but we did have to hunt down the winter layers that were still stuffed in the storage box in the basement. Until now, we hadn't even thought about it. Despite the sun, what we've been wearing for most of November would not work in the fresh wind that insisted on keeping temperatures below freezing. I'm glad it chilled down for today. The thought of a warm Thanksgiving is never appealing unless I'm vacationing in Hilton Head.

As always, it seemed like everyone from both Pilaf and Borger were at the game. We found Jim and Barb, and their family. They arrived early and had great seats below the guest's coaching box near the fifty yard line. There was still enough room for the four of us on the bleacher row just below them. Joel and Jessie were thrilled to be near their cousins.

Just before the game began Jimmy and Alice Giammalvo sat down in front of us. They came in with guests. It was clear after a few moments that they were British. Craig and Anne Linaker from the coastal town of Fleetwood, near the Scotland border, accepted the Giammalvo's invitation to come to America to join the festivities of our Thanksgiving. They were so excited to be a part of something they had only heard about through media and their friendship with Jimmy and Alice. It was fun to see Thanksgiving through this new perspective. We did have a little difficulty explaining American football to them since what they call "football" is what we call soccer. As confused as they were about what was happening on the field, they were able to grab onto the excitement of seeing the Pilaf Warriors play a valiant game. However, in the end, the Bulldogs hoisted the prized turkey trophy with a seven point win. We would later see the Linakers again after our own Thanksgiving dinner when we joined them for dessert at the Giammalvo's home. I hope they come and visit the store before they head back to England.

No turkey this year. It was all a part of Jennifer's plan to enjoy being at the game. After borrowing one extra crock pot from Barb, Jennifer slow-cooked a goose. Not ever having cooked a goose before, she was unaware of how much fat the bird would offer. Melted fat and juice from one of the crock pots overflowed onto the counter with evidence that Sammy had discovered it. Jessie discovered greasy paw prints leading out of the kitchen. Sure enough, Sammy was fast asleep in a stretched out position. He looked like he was smiling. Oh, great. There's no telling how much he was able to lap up or how his feline intestines will handle that unexpected goody. It must have been a fair amount. He never asked for his evening meal, nor did he take any interest in it when Joel put down his food bowl.

Friday, November 27, 2015, 9:02 a.m.

I don't know who is more stuffed from yesterday, me or Sammy. When I left for the store, Sammy's food bowl was still untouched.

It's raining this morning. I especially like experiencing the rain after a long dry period. The only music I listened to on the drive to the store was an atmospheric symphony of raindrops, conducted by the well-timed swipes of my windshield wipers. In fact, when I reached the store, I turned off the motor and closed my eyes for a moment to listen to the nuances of the sound of raindrops hitting the car. With no other distractions, I could hear the collective difference between the small raindrops and the less frequent, larger ones. Even more amazing was being able to tell what part of the car the larger drops struck.

Bailey's looked like a welcomed port in the foul weather. It would have been very easy to sit in the car for more than a few minutes, but I pictured Officer Caputo pulling up behind me with his lights going to yank my chain. That chance is pretty small on the morning after Thanksgiving, but the mere thought of it made me brave the rain.

The store had its characteristic chill back today. Because it was the day after Thanksgiving, I started a modest fire in the wood stove instead of pushing up the thermostat. The smell of the wood smoke combined with the crispiness of the air finally made it feel like we were entering into the holiday period. I must admit, I have not been thinking much about Christmas, or decorating for that matter. I have a list of store chores that need my attention before I can begin thinking about decorations.

Speaking of decorations, George's display should be up by now. If it dries out tonight, perhaps we will drive by to see if we can see anything new.

Uncle Ben was in earlier with Harry. They each put away a large cherry Danish and drank several cups of coffee before heading out. How they were able to do that after a huge Thanksgiving feast yesterday is beyond me. I nursed a single cup of coffee for most of the morning. I never seem to be hungry the morning after Thanksgiving, and I'm fine with that. Sammy has inadvertently joined me in discovering that there is a long lasting kind of satisfaction after holiday feasting.

Friday, November 27, 2015, 5:11 p.m.

What an eclectic day. We went from rain, to sunny, to breezy with thunderstorms, to the first visible snowflakes of the season. As I write this, the cold breeze is escorting snow flurries past the store windows. Nothing has yet accumulated. As weather-minded as I am, I was so busy getting the store ready for the Christmas season that I simply forgot to tune in to Stormy Windham's forecast for this weekend. That's unusual.

The store was fairly quiet until just after 1 o'clock this afternoon. It seemed like the cantankerous thunderstorm insisted on shaking everyone in Pilaf of out their turkey comas. The store went from hardly a whisper to a symphony of voices inside of one hour. It was fun to witness the transformation. Just when I thought I was seeing the crescendo, a few more people came in and joined the chorus. Things really ramped up when Jimmy and Alice Giammalvo escorted their British guests, Craig and Anne, into the store. I made sure to roll out the red carpet for them and told Gracie that Craig and Anne were our guests and to make sure they sampled everything that would give them a taste of life in Pilaf. Uncle Ben said that he made some gortons about a week ago. I called him and asked if he could bring a sample so that they could come back some morning before they returned to the U.K. Not even ten minutes later, Uncle Ben came into the mix with the gortons. He loves meeting new people. He carried on with them as if he had known Craig and Anne all of their lives. I was happy to hear Jimmy say that they would be in town through Monday morning. They were excited at the prospect of joining us for Sunday worship at our church.

George stopped by after the crowd thinned out. I told him that I was thinking about bringing our family out to see how many Christmas decorations we could find. George smiled, but I misinterpreted that smile. George told me not to expect to see anything different at his house this year. That surprised me. He always has something new up his sleeve. He said that he did have something new, but that I would not see it right now. When it comes to his Christmas decorations, George always puts on his best poker face.

I'm finally hungry again this evening after only snacking a little at lunch today when the Giammalvos and the Linakers were here. I have no idea what Jennifer is making, but it's always perfect for the day. With the cold winds escorting flurries past the windows, my guess is some kind of stew.

Saturday, November 28, 2015, 7:00 a.m.

Gracie offered to open the store this morning so that I could enjoy a relaxing Saturday morning with the family. My plan was to sleep in until at least 8 a.m., but I was wide awake at 6:30 a.m. At least the house is quiet right now. Jennifer and the kids are still sleeping and motionless as I write.

These are perfect moments to reflect and write. It's even better with a fresh cup of coffee in hand.

After a delightful family meal last night (yes, it was that the tastiest stew I've had since last winter), we did pile into the car to drive around Pilaf. I thought about parking at the town gazebo and walking the rest of the distance to George's house, but it seems like everyone forgot some aspect of their winter gear. Jennifer forgot a hat. Joel forgot his gloves. Jessica forgot her ear muffs. Admittedly, I didn't have any of those items and was thankful that everyone suggested staying toasty in the car. Jennifer dialed in a radio station that was playing all Christmas music. The snow flurries were wafting past the headlights, but none of it was accumulating. The cold winds were causing the snow to swirl on the roadway creating a strange fluid pattern on the pavement. It would have been easy to become mesmerized by it.

Despite the crispy winds arriving early in Pilaf, there was a fair amount of foot traffic frolicking around the decorated gazebo. The LED lights still looked as stunning as last year. From what Pilaf councilwoman, Pearl Barley, tells me, the town saved over a thousand dollars on their electric bill last December. Everything looked the same except for the addition of some lights on the cupola that were attached to a computer chip, adding color changes and action to the display.

We did drive by George's house and it looked grand, as usual. We timed it perfectly to hear Bing Crosby playing on his outdoor speakers, now one year old. I'll have to ask him if he took any measures to secure the receiving antennas from feathered or furry vandals. Joel looked out the window for the longest time, then finally asked if there was anything new in George's elaborate display. Joel has always been amazing with a keen sense of observation. Not much gets past him, even when you think he is not paying attention. He did not see anything new. I told him that George was planning something but had not yet been able to add it. The answer was good enough for Joel, but you could see a little disappointment as he and Jessie wrote something down on a small pad in the back seat. I, too, am waiting for George's change-up, even if it's something small.

It's still dark, but the deep blue hues of winter dawn are just starting to push through what appears to be a cloudy start. The snow flurries must have stopped overnight, but not before depositing a very light dusting on the deck and the sidewalk, but you can't see it anywhere else. It's a brisk 22°F. I hope we don't see a return of the warm and dry pattern. Joel and I need the chill to inspire us to decorate later this afternoon after I check in with Gracie at the store.

Sammy is curling around my leg and reminding me with his head jams that it's lap time.

We'll do that looking out the deck with a fresh cup of coffee.

Saturday, November 28, 2015, 7:02 p.m.

Let the Christmas season officially begin at the Rice home! Joel and Jessie have filled our home with their favorite Christmas tunes, alternating choices on the playlist that should last us through dinner. Jennifer is in the kitchen, rolling out homemade pizza dough. The kids were thrilled when she took their suggestion for pizza. There are very few pizza places around that compare with the way Jennifer makes her homemade pizza. My mouth is watering just anticipating it. The only one that comes to mind is Riccardi's thin crust pizza. When we order carry-out pizza, Riccardi's is the only place we all like almost as much as Jennifer's.

I did not spend much time at Bailey's today. Gracie had everything under control, as usual. In fact, she started adding Christmas decorations around the store. Some of it I recognized from the well-worn box that I store in the attic. Gracie must have braved all of those dusty cobwebs and crawled up through the hatch in the second floor ceiling. I'm impressed. Gracie screams at the smallest spider that she imagines is chasing her. Some of the decorations must have come from her own collection at home since I don't recognize them, but I liked what she added to the mix.

Donald Buckley stopped in for a brief visit. Somehow, we started talking about desserts. I learned that Donald is not a fan of pie except for one particular kind. I guessed apple for the obvious reason, and I was right. He says that he likes all kinds of fruit, but the minute a crust is added, the fruit's appeal is gone. Apple pie is different. While I can't relate to that specifically, I can understand it. A good example is Jessie's love for orange juice. Try to give her an orange, though, and you'll get the biggest frown you've ever seen. Oranges are definite no-gos. With the end of that conversation, Gracie kicked me out of my own store. (She's the only one who can do that.)

I returned home where Joel was patiently waiting for me. All of the boxes and bags that contained the outdoor Christmas decorations surrounded him, ready to bring outside. The LED strips that we assembled in numerous three-foot sections were going to be the highlight of our decorating challenge. The computer controlled lights worked in theory, but would they work once assembled on the roofline? Time would tell. Those strips went up first. Everything else was secondary. Before dark, we plugged it all in. It all worked exactly the way it was supposed to. Joel was clearly elated and looked forward to programming the roofline lights. After pizza, we'll all stand outside while Joel shows us some of the fun lighting tricks that he learned from Aaron, the tech guru at church.

Sunday, November 29, 2015, 7:38 a.m.

A thick, hard frost greeted Sammy and me as we both looked out the window. Once I sat down, he wasted no time jumping up onto my legs. I could feel the chill of the soft pads of his paws and he tried to find a position that would give him the quickest warm-up. That benefitted me just as much as him. Everyone will stir soon to get ready for church. Uncle Ben's group study series on the book of Colossians before the worship service has truly been outstanding. It has been a while since I was so energized by our Sunday morning group study. A few in our group still call it "Sunday school" out of habit, even though Pastor O'Connor changed the name to update its contemporary image shortly after our family returned to Pilaf from the city. We still do the same thing that others arriving at 9:30 a.m. on Sunday morning have done for decades, even centuries - to study God's Word with intentionality. Sunday school, group study, classroom time, call it what you will. However you label the gathering of eager followers of the Lord Jesus Christ to study God's Word will never change the wonderful growth that awaits those who want to draw closer to God.

Uncle Ben has been trying to get Harry Buser to come to the group study for some time now. Harry is always there for the service, but he hasn't ever participated in the group study in the hour before. Harry is a very private man, but Uncle Ben seems to relate to him in ways which others have not. That's easy to see when he is enjoying a cup of coffee with Harry at their preferred table-for-two by the front window. It would be fun to have Harry at the group study. My guess is that he would contribute in a special way.

Officer Caputo was on duty last night when he knocked at the front door. Was I in some kind of mischievous trouble again? As much as I would have liked to peek into George's house once more to see what's new in his Christmas depot, I restrained myself remembering the embarrassment of Jim's siren and flashing blue lights last year, alerting the neighbors of my innocent curiosity. When I opened the door, he had a smirk on his face. His finger pointed up at the roofline and he simply said, "Nice lights."

I assumed that he was making reference to our LED roofline. He was. Then he asked me if I had programmed it to get his attention. I didn't understand what he meant until I grabbed a jacket, put something on my feet and followed him down the driveway. What I saw shocked me so much that I started laughing. Jim started laughing just as hard. Joel was getting very good and very creative with programming the LED strips. Our roofline looked like a police car in full pursuit of Pilaf's public enemy number one. While he did kindly ask me to have Joel change the display to something less alarming to passers-by, Officer Caputo's curiosity was piqued and wanted to see how the family computer in the living room was used to program the lights. He could not stay long enough for Joel to show him some of the key elements, so he asked if he could come back sometime for a better look.

Even with the enthusiasm that Jim showed, Joel was a little frightened about the visit. Before he left, Jim reassured Joel that he was not in any trouble. Nonetheless, he did gently suggest that programming something different would prevent unsuspecting drivers coming up over the hill from getting an unneeded rush of adrenalin. I could tell that Jim had yet one more story that he could put into that book he may one day write about being Pilaf's beloved police chief.

Sunday, November 29, 2015, 5:30 p.m.

It was so much fun having our new British friends with us for church. Not only did they come to Uncle Ben's group study, they actively participated and shared in ways that gave us a wonderful perspective on the Scripture passages that we studied. They had a way of making us feel like royalty with their delightful British accent which made us feel like we were in the presence of a special, royal family. Everyone I know thinks that a British accent is eloquent and mellifluous, the kind that adds an air of nobility. I couldn't help thinking about how Craig and Anne must be processing our American Midwest accent. Do they think ours is delightful to take in, or do they see it as harsh as it would seem to us compared to theirs? I was bold enough to ask them, but that opportunity would not come until the afternoon.

Having Craig and Anne with us for worship made us realize just how small this ball of dirt we call Earth truly is. Fleetwood, England isn't such a far away place when you consider the greatness of the universe. Many of us in Pilaf will probably never get to travel to Europe, but the special bond we now have with the Linakers makes their hometown now seem very, very close in our hearts. The more we learned about Fleetwood, the more we all realized that their little seacoast town near the Scotland border is strikingly similar to our cozy little town of Pilaf. The only discernible differences would be Pilaf's absence of an ocean, the smell of salt water, and a steady ocean breeze. Craig and Anne did not seem to mind that we are landlocked for more than a hundred miles, and surrounded by oceans of rich, rolling farmland.

Many of us did not want to leave the church after service concluded, including Pastor O'Connor, who took a shine to their British accent. Likewise, they loved Pastor O'Connor's Australian accent, one that has not waned a bit over the decades that he and his wife spent in both Ethiopia as a missionaries, and twice as many years as a pastor in the United States. Uncle Ben, Harry Buser, George the mailman, Jim and Barb, the Giammalvos and their guests were the last ones remaining in the atrium when I had a grand idea. I invited them all to Bailey's where I offered to heat up some of Gracie's corn chowder accompanied by sandwiches. I was delighted when everyone said yes. I could give Jennifer a break from the kitchen and treat our family and friends.

Bailey's has such life on afternoons like today. Oh, it has a life all its own during the week, but on Sunday, it's a different kind of life when I use the store to entertain guests for a cozy after church lunch. I don't have the usual chores to attend to. The atmosphere is relaxing and joyful. Since Bailey's is closed on Sunday, not a single person, not even a wayward out-of-towner, has ever tried to come in thinking that we were open for business despite the cars in the parking lot.

After lunch, Jim suggested showing the Linakers the Jasmine Creek footpath. About half of us suited up for a short walk to see the creek. Craig and Anne were eager to take in as much of Pilaf as they could since their time here would come to a close on Tuesday morning. We made it down as far as the spot where I removed that horrible thorny vine last year. I was surprised to see that another shoot had not attempted to grow back. In fact, what did take its place was a very large, pink-hued mushroom. I know of only two people in Pilaf who might be able to tell me if it was the edible variety. One of them is Gabby Sauerkraut. She made a phenomenal mushroom soup for the church potluck a few months ago. Nobody knew until we all moved on to dessert that she personally harvested the mushrooms before our weather pattern dried out. That clearly made some people uneasy, but I tried reassuring everyone that Mrs. Sauerkraut has been doing that since she was a little girl. Her mother and father taught her everything she knows about mushrooms. If the truth be known, I wouldn't mind if some avoided her soup. That would mean more for me as Mrs. Sauerkraut never likes to head home with leftovers. She is most pleased when she can serve others to the finish line.

The creek was flowing slowly and there was no ice visible anywhere yet. Despite the chill in the air since Thanksgiving, it was nowhere near cold enough to cool the creek after our extended warm fall pattern.

On our way back to the store, I noticed a couple walking some distance ahead of us heading toward the town gazebo. While I could not be certain, it sure looked like Mr. Rayburn and Miss Miller walking together. Interesting.

Monday, November 30, 2015, 6:44 a.m.

The pre-dawn moon captured my attention as I drove to the store this morning. It shared the sky with fast-moving, low, puffy clouds. The contrast was attractive. There was no wind at the surface, so it was interesting that the clouds were moving so fast. Perhaps that's what made it so enchanting. I'll have to pay attention when Stormy comes on this morning. Perhaps something is brewing.

The kids were quieter than usual on Sunday night. I think they were simply exhausted from an afternoon playing with their cousins after church, not to mention the long and brisk walk down the Jasmine Creek footpath. I think they had the most fun escorting Amaroo, Jim and Barb's golden retriever, to various interesting nooks just off the path. Come to think of it, it was probably much more like Amaroo escorting (okay, dragging) the kids to the nooks that he thought were worthy of his time.

I still have some of Uncle Ben's gortons in the back room refrigerator. As soon as I attend to a couple more items, my intention is to make myself an English muffin topped with the last remains. As long as I have cherry Danish in the case (which I do), I'm safe with making the gortons disappear.

Sammy seems to be back on schedule. He greeted me in the kitchen and was trying to butter me up for his first meal. I told him that he was too early, but that 9 o'clock would come soon. Call me crazy, but I think he actually understood what I was trying to tell him. Jennifer also seems to think that he knows far more of our language than he lets on. There are plenty of days where I wonder. He smiled and trotted away.

There's a new digital monitor facing out to passers-by from inside the Pilaf Credit Union this morning. I don't think it was there yesterday, so I'm assuming someone placed it there late yesterday so that Monday traffic would see it. Because it was dark, I certainly did. There was some smaller print that I could not read while I was passing by the bank, but the main message was hard to miss: 25 Days To Christmas. I'm assuming they were advertising their Christmas Savings Club. Most banks saw their height of popularity peak in the 1970s. You don't hear about them all too often except at local credit unions. According to Lynne Cotter, the president of Pilaf Credit Union, 72% of all credit unions in the United States still have a Christmas savings club and that consumer interest in these "clubs" is still steady. Of course, they are not really clubs, but simply a name to rally people around the idea of saving for specific periods of time. He said that most people who open up these accounts actually start them in March.

That sign with the giant "25" reminded me of another number I've seen pop up in the kid's room. I have no idea what these numbers mean and I've been meaning to ask Joel and Jessie what they are, but every time I remember, they are either out playing, in school, or sleeping. It started a few weeks ago. Both of them had a giant, colorful zero on the whiteboards that each one has in their room. It almost looked like each was trying to outdo the other to make it the most colorful and artful zero possible. It stayed at zero for a long time. About a week ago, I started seeing that change. At first it was "2," then a few days ago "5." Last night, I walked into their rooms to check on them after they fell asleep. Both whiteboards had a colorful "11" written on them. There was no other notation anywhere around them, and consequently no clues as to whatever was increasing. It has to be simple since they are both in agreement.

Monday, November 30, 2015, 4:43 p.m.

Stormy nailed it. He talked about a fast-moving jet stream shift that was strong enough to potentially change our dry weather pattern thus far. He gave us the science behind what we were about to see. I'm certain now that it was directly connected to the odd sight of having so many clouds zipping by when there wasn't a whip of wind pushing as much as a blade of grass anywhere when I looked at the pre-sunrise sky. I like telling people that I seem to have a weather-sense. Stormy would agree, telling the masses that everyone has a weather-sense if we take the time to observe and watch, using all of our senses.

After sunrise, the sky looked as normal as any late November day could be. People came and went into the store just like any other Monday. Then something seemed odd. I finally realized that I was turning on lights that I normally don't reach for until twilight. It was approaching 1 o'clock in the afternoon.

Since then, drizzle and fog moved in, but no heavy rain as one might expect. The darkness mimicked the approach of a summertime thunderstorm. I kept looking out the window expecting something more than just drizzle and fog.

Being curious, I checked to see if the porch thermometer was showing any noteworthy trend. Not really. It was just barely 40°F before noon. It's 38°F now.

Despite no change in the temperature from earlier today, the darkness compelled me to start a fire in the woodstove. The dampness gradually left the store and the dark skies didn't seem so foreboding. There's also something to be said for dark daytime skies at this time of year. The Christmas decorations, especially the lighted ones, take on a comforting glow. Granted, not everything is up, but Gracie decorated enough to be noticed in a way that would have been much less visible with sunny skies. It's what I've always called the cozy cocoon effect.

Jimmy Giammalvo brought the Linakers in for one final visit before they head back to the UK. I wanted to send them back with a batch of Uncle Ben's gortons, but without refrigeration, I would hate to envision the result nearly twenty hours later. I had to settle for sending them back with a jar of Mary Woisnet's elderberry jelly. There isn't a soul in America who can make jellies like her. Mary is nearing the title of centenarian, but that doesn't seem to slow her down. A part of me wants to stash at least one of those precious jars of jelly in a temperature controlled vault for safe keeping and a special occasion. Mary jokingly tells everyone that once she hits that one-hundred year mark, she is aiming on taking flight and leaving her well-aged body behind. She is teaching everyone in Pilaf how to live life to the very fullest and to ignore the number of candles on each year's cake.

Tuesday, December 1, 2015, 9:40 a.m.

December. There's something likable about simply saying the word, isn't there? Even as the skies host less and less daylight and the temperatures get colder and colder, the month gets more and more exciting. That has forever been the case regardless of anyone's age. I need to get Joel and his cousin, Drake, back together to add some Christmas decorating fun at Bailey's.

By now, the Linakers must be getting ready to fly back to the UK. Their first leg was to Boston this morning. With Jimmy opening up his market, Alice brought them to the airport. To account for a lengthy check-in time, they said that they were going to set their alarm for 4:00 a.m. The air is still cold, damp, and drizzly. Perhaps it's the atmosphere's way of easing them back into the typical English weather which awaits them. Both Jimmy and Alice will be tired today, I'm sure, but thrilled to have hosted their friends for Thanksgiving. I'm glad that we were able to be a part of their visit. I hope we get to see them again soon.

Harry came into the store looking for Uncle Ben early this morning. He said that while he did not make specific plans to meet him today, he took a chance that Uncle Ben might come in for coffee and a Danish as he often does. Harry waited for a while, sipping on a cup of fresh coffee. When it was clear that Uncle Ben was not planning on coming today, Harry paid for his coffee and started for the door. He looked troubled. The Spirit of God quickened me to ask him a question, any question, to prevent him from reaching the door. I asked him if he liked apple pie. What? Why did I ask that? As crazy as that was, it must have been the right thing. Harry turned around and his countenance changed as if someone turned on a light switch. He said he loved apple pie and asked me if I had any in the pie rack. Five minutes later, Harry was sitting opposite me at the counter, savoring a slice of caramel crumb apple pie and another mug of coffee.

Harry offered typical, pleasant small talk until the pie was nearly gobbled up. That's when he asked me the question that has really pressing on his heart and mind.

"Do you ever feel like God is so distant, that He seems unreal, untouchable?"

Compared to all the light chatter that led up to this question, this was a bombshell. I could relate to that question, though. It was only a handful of years ago that I was so wrapped up in my own schedule, that the things of God began to feel like distant theory. I had to admit to Harry that it was of my own doing.

Harry didn't feel so troubled now that he knew that someone else could relate, even a little. Our conversation returned to apple pie. He relished it so much that I decided to cut myself a slice. Indeed, it was excellent with coffee.

Tuesday, December 1, 2015, 6:55 p.m.

Jimmy and Alice gave me the flight tracking link for the Linaker's flight back to London. Right now, they are somewhere between Gander, Newfoundland and Narsarsauq, Greenland, some 300 miles away from any land mass.

The drizzle never gave up today. Temperatures were stable at 44°F. It was a good day to get busy preparing the store for Christmas.

George came in for lunch. He asked if Gracie had made any corn chowder recently. Unfortunately, no. We wiped it out on Sunday when we hosted our friends for lunch after church. In one way, I hate to ask Gracie to make some more. On the other hand, she says that she best operates when serving in her area of giftedness. Corn chowder is definitely one of them. I made some tomato bisque earlier and was able to convince George to try a bowl with a grilled cheese sandwich.

I asked George if I could borrow a few of his Christmas CDs. Sometimes I like a little more control over the music that my customers hear in the background as they browse, shop, or eat. It's not that the all-Christmas formats on the radio don't live up to my expectation, but there are times when I'm in the mood for a particular genre of holiday melodies. I'll have to keep closer track of how the weather dictates what I select. My guess is that there is a connection.

I did ask George if he was done adding to his decorations this year. He told me that he might be ready by Thursday or Friday. That's late for him. I haven't a clue what could take so long to install. There certainly isn't a single clue that I've been able to see from the outside. I dare not look in his window, day or night, unless Officer Caputo is with me.

Jennifer is making sloppy Joes for tonight, a real family crowd-pleaser. There was another scent occasionally mixing in with the sloppy Joes. At first, I could not tell what it was. As the aroma became stronger, my guess was her Mount Mansfield apple pie. We named it that after a vacation in Vermont. Upon seeing Vermont's tallest mountain peak from a distance, Joel and Jessie pointed to it and said that it looked like Mom's apple pie crust. The closer we got to Mount Mansfield, the greater the resemblance. It's a great story that we all enjoy sharing when people ask us why we call it Mount Mansfield apple pie.

In my humble opinion, Jennifer's apple pie is second to none. Granted, I've not had many others, so my frame of reference is somewhat limited. We always hear about Miss Miller's apple pie as being heavenly from all the teachers in the academy. Uncle Ben claims to make a good one, too. Perhaps we ought to entertain a Pilaf apple pie baking competition. I like the sound of this.

Wednesday, December 2, 2015, 7:38 a.m.

After two solid days of dark gray skies, the Pilaf sunrise is stunning this morning. It actually sent me to my journal so that I could capture it in words. The sun is sending three shafts of light through the east window, the angle almost parallel to the floor. With a nice, little fire going in the wood stove, there is just enough wood smoke in the air to see the three shafts like three theatrical spotlights. Yet, the source for each of the shafts is a single point of light. Sounds like a great sermon illustration for Pastor O'Connor.

I've given more thought to Harry's deep question. Perhaps this is why Uncle Ben has been trying to get Harry to join us during our group study time at church. We've been studying the epistle to the Colossians. Almost from the get go, the apostle Paul presents Jesus as the visible manifestation of the invisible God, God's very Son who put on the flesh of a human being. There certainly must be a way to place handles on this Scripture so that Harry can grab a hold of it.

It's great to see the sunshine back, but it's interesting how it makes the Christmas decorations inside the store fade into more of a subtle visual background. I'm good with that, though. That's what nighttime is for, and there is plenty of that during this season as we approach the longest night of the year in a couple of weeks. I'll be curious to see what kind of weather pattern awaits us. Stormy's forecast will be on during the 8 a.m. news block. Time to turn the radio on so that I won't miss it. It's great to have Stormy's face still on my memory from last December's surprise encounter at the Pilaf gazebo. I wonder if we will see him swing by again this year? It's fun to think that a voice which is so easily recognized in Pilaf can suddenly materialize in the flesh. He really does exist, and doesn't live as an entity inside my radio.

It's fun seeing Pilaf come to Christmas life. I had to run back to Bailey's to retrieve my cell phone after dinner last night. I assumed it was on the lunch counter, and that is exactly where I found it. Joel and Jessie surprised me when they asked if they could come for the ride. Both had finished their homework, so I was delighted to have them with me for the quick trip. They sat quietly in the back seat pointing at all the new Christmas lights that we saw on the trip down. During the drive back to the house, they did the same curious thing except they had a yellow legal pad out. They were jotting things down as we drove back home. No explanation was offered, nor did I ask what they were doing.

Wednesday, December 2, 2015, 5:02 p.m.

I just turned the store's main lights off as well as the bright, neon open sign facing out the porch window. I like it better than the cardboard sign that I had as a carry over from Frank Bailey's days here.

Mrs. Krumm was in today after school. She lacked her usual focus. After meandering up and down the aisles for what seemed like fifteen minutes, she came up to the counter with some sugar wafer cookies. She then asked if she could have that last slice of apple pie in the pie case. I'm used to seeing her come up with some really oddball combinations, but this one struck me as being very odd. I was actually tempted to ask if everything was okay, but I convinced myself that it was just a Mrs. Krummism. She nodded her thanks and was on her way out the door when she dropped her bag. Apologizing, she picked it up, shook her head at her clumsiness and walked out the front door. I couldn't put my finger on it, but I just didn't like the sequence of events I just witnessed. I'll ask the kids to keep a close eye on her at school.

It was a beautiful day. The sun was bright all day and there was a light, but mild breeze. It seems as though we are heading back into the mild and dry pattern, but Stormy did warn everyone not to get used to it. That warm and dry pattern is tougher to keep in place during the month of December. More flurries are in the picture for later this week.

Thursday, December 3, 2015, 5:50 a.m.

The alluring aroma of Jennifer's Dutch baby pancake in the kitchen reminded me that she made Joel and Jessie's breakfast ahead of time last night while Officer Caputo and I were in the living room watching Joel program the roofline lights after dinner. Jim asked if certain sequences could be programmed. I didn't think so, but Joel was quick to say yes to just about every wild combination that Jim thought of. Sure enough, after executing many of Jim's requests, we would step outside and see an impressive display. The only thing off limits is making our roofline look like a police car with a speeder pulled over on the side of the road. Jim wanted to see more, but had to excuse himself and asked if he might come back again on Friday evening. Joel was naturally thrilled with the prospect.

The artistic numbers drawn on Joel and Jessie's whiteboards is now up to 21. I'm certainly curious to know what this number is all about, but they are still sound asleep and won't be up for another twenty minutes. Even if I was home when they arose, my guess is that they would want more time to wake up before being asked anything. I'll eventually get the story.

Thursday, December 3, 2015, 6:21 p.m.

It was one of those days when catching up seemed like an impossible task from the moment I turned the key and walked inside the front door at Bailey's. Something seemed amiss, but I could not quite put my finger on what that might be. After turning on the lights and starting a pot of coffee, Maureen Whittles arrived with my order of breakfast pastries from Giammalvo's Market. Her familiar smile reassured me. Whatever happened after her visit, regardless of how crazy the day became, would surely work out in the end. What a coup it would be if I could convince Maureen to join Gracie here at Bailey's. Alas, I'll have to admire her loyalty to the Giammalvos. I've heard her marvel many times that Jimmy actually pays her for what she would easily do just for fun.

      The air was unusually crisp inside Bailey's. It was not that cold outside. The porch thermometer read 31°F when I initially walked in. Having installed one of those new WiFi-connected thermostats a few months ago, not once have I needed to adjust it in the morning. Then again, the furnace has not had much of a workout thus far. I'm sure that will eventually change. It always does. A walk over to the thermostat made it spring to life when I approached the dial. It indicated that it was sending a signal to the furnace to warm things up to 65°F, but that it was 56°F and the furnace was not responding. Sure enough, the furnace was not coming to life. The pilot light was fine. Cycling the breaker did nothing. It was time to call the experts. Until the repairman arrived, it was time to stoke up the woodstove a wee bit.

      George stopped in before heading to the post office. He seemed a little impatient when I asked him when we could expect to see this year's Christmas twist to his decorations. He admitted to the fact that he was a little behind this year, but there was good reason for it. George assured me that it would be "soon."

The furnace repairman finally drove up just before lunch. Fortunately, the cold December winds have not arrived and the woodstove took enough of Bailey's chill to make customers comfortable. Since there was a lull in the foot traffic, I asked Gracie to mind the store while I took a short walk. I ended up at the top of the street where George lives and decided to walk by even though I knew that there was nothing new to see, or so I thought. As I approached the house, there was a rather large box that had been delivered on his front porch. Could this be the item for which George was waiting? The entire neighborhood was so quiet that you could have heard a kitten walking through the grass across the street. Surely, walking up onto George's porch to see this curious box for a few seconds would be okay. No sooner did I climb the seven brick stairs with the box fully in view that I heard the sound of car tires on the pavement behind me. I had a sinking feeling. It was Officer Caputo, again. This time he did not send me through the porch roof with his siren and lights, but he did roll down his window and stare at me for a moment. I felt my face turn red as I just shrugged my shoulders. His window rolled back up, staring at me the entire time. He then

pulled away with what looked like a miniature
smirk. Great. Busted again. I'm sure that somehow,
George will be informed of my cat-like curiosity.

I returned to the store as the lunch crowd
was building. It was busier than normal and Gracie
needed help. I covered the counter orders while
Gracie took phone calls and assembled the take-out
orders for soup and sandwiches. Even brother Jim
showed up for a corned beef sandwich, one of his
favorites. By half-past noon, every table was busy,
and it wasn't even Friday, usually my busiest day. I
felt suddenly warm, but I thought it was because I
was running around at warp speed. Then the
furnace repairman suddenly appeared from the
basement and gave me the thumbs up. That's why it
suddenly felt delightfully warm.

He told me that the fan had failed. He had
the exact model I needed in the truck and installed
it. Then he gave me the invoice. $178 for the fan
and $58 for labor? That seemed a little high, but
then again, I've not needed any furnace repairs in
recent memory. I tried not to grumble while I pulled
out my checkbook and ledger to pay him. I offered
him a sandwich or a drink, but he said there was
another customer whose furnace wasn't working.
He did take a pop for the road, then he was gone.
Gracie could tell that I wasn't happy about the bill,
but she assured me that the repairman had no idea.

Apparently, in the mad rush to take care of
so many things, I never saw George come in a drop

off my bundle of mail. It was sitting at the corner of the counter not far from where I was writing a check for $236. An envelope from the Pilaf library was on the top of the stack. Was I overdue on a book? That's all I would need to add to this already busy day. I opened the envelope. It was a check made out to Bailey's for a catering job we did for them in late October. I forgot all about it. The check was for $236. Even in the crazy set of the day's events, some of it of my own doing, God was still extraordinarily gracious to me.

Friday, December 4, 2015, 10:04 a.m.

It was two years ago today that I walked into Bailey's, not as a customer, but as the owner. So much has gone on in this town since our family has returned, but not the kind of things that make the nightly news in the city. The things that happen here are what gives a town the kind of character that make it a fun place to live. The noise of the big city made it difficult to find real life unfolding. When it happens, it's always in the background. There's a danger in getting caught up in the urgent pace of life. Eventually, the special moments of life go completely unnoticed. Getting off the hamster wheel is nearly impossible. After a while, you don't even know that you are on it. There are no hamster wheels in Pilaf, and plenty of real life unfolding every day.

Here's an example. George's new twist added to his Christmas decorations is a big deal every year here in Pilaf. Everyone starts to speculate about it even before our Thanksgiving meals are digested. If George were to do the same thing in the big city, not many people would notice. The few that did notice would not likely care all that much. His decorations might even be stolen if they were not anchored down somehow.

Speaking of George, he was my very first customer on the day I opened Bailey's under my watch. He was also my first customer today, exactly two years later. We exchanged pleasantries as he had a cup of coffee, but that was all. I was expecting him to say something about my visit to his porch, but he said nothing about it. I hope that Officer Caputo forgot to tell him.

Uncle Ben met Harry for a cup of coffee. Uncle Ben surprised me when he asked for the apple-cinnamon muffin instead of his usual cherry Danish. He figures that eating anything made with apples will make it feel more like Christmas since the weather pattern isn't doing the job yet. I told him he should have come yesterday when the store's furnace broke down. Both of them stayed at their favorite table for about an hour. It was clear that they were deep in conversation, ignoring the foot traffic that walked past them. Uncle Ben had his Bible open for a little while. Judging from the page stack on both sides, he was in a New Testament epistle. Perhaps it was Colossians.

Friday, December 4, 2015, 10:25 p.m.

It was such a delightful day of celebration. Most everyone who came into Bailey's knew that it was my second anniversary. Those who did not were quickly told. It turned into an all-day festival. Again, that's one of those special moments that is recognized and gives Pilaf its unique character.

Things were slow after the lunch crowd left. I took advantage of yet another atmospheric gift of sunshine, and no wind, to take a walk to the town gazebo. Even with sunshine accenting the still somewhat green lawns, the town square looked festive. This was the Christmas recharge that I needed. It is only a matter of time before December snows give the square a special ambiance. It seems like the whole town comes out to enjoy it when it happens.

My thoughts turned toward Stormy Windham. I was standing in the same spot where I heard his distinct voice last December. After meeting him, I can no longer remember what I thought he might look like based only on his radio forecasts. It was then that I received a revelation. Stormy almost seemed like some surreal entity out there, in some other dimension, before our paths crossed. Meeting him face-to-face changed all of that. Stormy was no longer an untouchable, unreachable entity. I thought of Harry's deep, probing question. In fact, I could still hear it echoing in my head: "Do you ever feel like God is a so distant, that He seems unreal, untouchable?"

Stormy gave me his email address last year. Until now, and wanting to respect his privacy and earn his trust, I had no reason to use it. Because Stormy is a follower of Christ, I'm sure he would want to help bring a Scripture passage to life for a struggling believer. That passage comes from the first chapter of Colossians and essentially talks about Jesus as the visible image of the invisible God. I'll send him an email this weekend to see if he is available.

Tomorrow is the day we will get our Christmas tree. I announced it before dinner.

Jennifer joked with me that I should have done that after dinner. The amount of excitement released is similar to winding a spring-loaded toy far too tightly. I must admit, I do get a kick out of it. It took extra time to coax both Joel and Jessie to eat their dinner.

Jim and Barb called earlier to invite us over for dessert and board games tomorrow night. That's always a great way to end the work week. I'm also curious to see if Drake decorated the pine tree at the end of the driveway with blue lights. I haven't heard anything about that this year.

Saturday, December 5, 2015, 9:01 a.m.

It's raining. That's what everyone is talking about as customers come into the store. My guess is that the rain has been steady since it started late last night. We've had quick gully-gushers here and there since late September and October, but no long-lasting, continuous rainy spells like this. I think that it's going to rain all day. My clue comes from a special barometer. It's the barometer that my Uncle Arthur owned when he lived on the farm.

Nowadays, it proudly hangs on one of Bailey's support beams. It has been there for exactly two years and one day. It was one of the first things that I hung when I stepped inside of Bailey's as its new owner.

The needle has been in a slow fall all morning. Fast fall means fast changes. Slow fall means slow changes. I remember that general rule of thumb from Stormy's radio forecasts. That's why I think the rain will be falling for a while.

I find it fascinating how this rainy day is embraced. Everyone is in a wonderful mood. That's because it is in contrast to the months of mainly dry and mild weather. Likewise, if you have months of wet weather, the first sunny and warm day is celebrated. We humans were designed to enjoy variety in everything, I suspect. It's how God wired us.

Joel and Jessie were each having a bowl of oatmeal when I left the house earlier this morning. Jessie was telling me that Mrs. Krumm hasn't been in school for a few days. There has been a substitute teacher in her class since mid-week. I hope I see Mr. Rayburn today to ask him how she is. She did not look herself when she was here on Wednesday.

Uncle Ben was in earlier and stayed for a while. I told him that Harry asked me that deep, probing question about God. Uncle Ben confirmed my suspicion that he was trying to help Harry in recent weeks. I told him about the revelation that I received regarding our local radio meteorologist Stormy Windham. Uncle Ben was thrilled that I had his contact information and thought my idea would likely help Harry grab on to a big spiritual truth. I still have to send Stormy an email about this. I have no reason to believe that he won't answer.

I asked Gracie if she would close the store this afternoon so that I could begin the hunt for a Christmas tree. She said that she would under one condition - that I would pick up a small, live, two-foot tree for Bailey's. I like that idea. Perhaps my lighting engineers, Joel and Drake, can help Gracie decorate it next week.

As far back as I can remember, I don't ever recall going out to get a Christmas tree in the rain. This could become a memorable adventure. I'll stop by the house to make sure that Joel and Jessie are with me to share the experience.

Saturday, December 5, 2015, 6:40 p.m.

Did I use the word adventure? Our Christmas tree search was all of that, and more.

I left Bailey's at 2:30 p.m. It was still raining, and it was cold. On the way home, some of the houses that I passed had their Christmas candle lights illuminated in the windows. They were easily visible against the dark, gray sky. Some of them caught my eye because their light refracted in unique patterns through the raindrops on my windshield. When I approached our house, I saw one window with one candle showing in the living room. It was easy to assume that the kids found the boxes of Christmas decorations and were ready to get a tree on which to hang them. It wasn't hard to convince them to get ready for the car ride to the tree farm.

Jennifer scrambled to make sure the kids were armed with their waterproof rain gear. I thought it was overkill, but I didn't say anything. Jennifer retreated to the kitchen to start dinner, and we waltzed out the door and piled into the car.

The drive to the Christmas tree farm was full of joy and anticipation. Jessie tuned the radio to one of the stations playing Christmas music. The atmosphere was grand. Twenty minutes later, we arrived at the tree farm, picked a pull-cart big enough for our tree and a second smaller one. Off we went. Every ten steps or so, I stopped to admire a tree as a perfect specimen. Both Joel and Jessie gave me a thumbs down. In another ten or twenty paces, the scene repeated. After passing up more than a half-dozen trees that looked fine to me, I knew this would not be a quick task. We walked down to the end of the first row of trees, nearly three-hundred yards, and we did not have a tree in our pull-cart. We started heading back down the second row where the scene repeated numerous times. Not even halfway back, I felt something awful on my right foot, followed immediately by my left. I didn't want to look down, but I did. The cold, wet mud was starting to ooze through my sneakers. I asked Joel and Jessie if their feet were dry. Not only were they dry, but they said that they were nice and toasty. So much for overkill.

As uncomfortable as my feet were, I refused to allow it to squelch the joy the kids were having while looking for the perfect tree. I hoped that we would find it quickly though. We were close to the end of the second row when they both pointed to what they believed was the perfect tree. I must admit, I'm glad we didn't settle for the first one that I liked.

There came a new challenge. I forgot to bring the hand saw. I had to slosh all the way back to the car, retrieve the saw, and walk back to the tree. At this point, the muddy water was wicking up toward my knees. Since I was getting dirty quickly, I volunteered to saw the tree down. Normally, Joel would ask to help, but the muddy ground was a sufficient deterrent. Because I had to kneel low to get a good cut, now the cold, muddy water was wicking up my thighs. What a sight. When I stood up after felling the tree, I couldn't help noticing that Joel and Jessie were trying to hold back giggles.

Our tasks were not yet complete. As miserably cold as I was, I needed to find the two-foot tree for Bailey's. The kids had no real personal interest in approving or disapproving my choice for that tree, so I made a quick choice, chopped it down, and added it to our pull-cart.

We paid for our trees, tied them to our roof rack, and started driving home in the heavier rain which was now mixing with big, wet snowflakes. The car heater did little to warm my cold, wet, and muddy legs. Thankfully, there was a towel that I draped over the seat to save our upholstery from having to be professionally cleaned.

The kids asked if I could drive past Uncle Ben's house to see if his decorations were up. It was not the most direct route home, but far be it from me to deny such a joyful request. As we approached Uncle Ben's house, a squirrel bolted out in front of the car. I swerved hard to miss Rocky. Rocky survived. I can't even remember if Uncle Ben's decorations were up or not. I was ready to head home and take a hot shower.

Upon arriving home, we prepared to unload the trees from the roof rack when I realized there was an awful lot of give in the twine holding the cargo down. That's when I realized that we lost the two-foot tree somewhere between the farm and home. At least we had our tree. I'll backtrack and look for the small one later.

I have not seen Sammy since we came home. I wonder if he was alarmed at the scene. Perhaps he is having flashbacks of last year's "tree attack."

Once the tree was standing tall and stable in the living room, I retreated for a long, hot shower while Joel and Jessie started decorating. I feel much better now. Jennifer's Chicken Divan is filling the house with a wonderful aroma. I'm ready for a wonderful meal. Dessert will be at Jim and Barb's house, although I have to admit, I thought more than once about cancelling our plans after our eventful afternoon.

Sunday, December 6, 2015, 8:30 a.m.

Sammy actually woke me this morning with a gentle nose-to-nose touch. Surely cats must know what they are doing. Why else would he want to smell my face? I don't think I had any lingering traces of the chocolate covered bacon that I sampled at Jim and Barb's last night. Bacon or not, this is rather unusual behavior for Sammy.

Sammy seemed pleased that I was getting up. I followed as he led me downstairs and to the sliding glass door in the back. I shouldn't have been surprised with what I saw, but I was. The landscape was white with fresh snow, about three inches of what appeared to be a heavy and wet variety. When the kids woke from their sleep, gleeful screaming filled the house. I hope the snow stays around long enough for Joel and Jessie to enjoy it it this afternoon.

Saturday evening at Jim and Barb's was the usual blast. The first thing we saw was their little pine tree at the driveway's entrance all lit up. It was blue!... then it faded... and morphed to green!... then it faded... and morphed to red! What a great idea. Drake has his blue LED lights every so often and was fully satisfied. Jim liked the variety of seeing blue, red, and green. The transitions in between the color cycles were also different. Sometimes they faded. At other times, the new color chased the old one out from top to bottom. Then there was one that looked like it glittered to the new color. Apparently, Drake did all of the programming. They had help from Aaron, our church lighting director. Aaron's help was invaluable since neither Jim nor Drake had any idea where to start on this project.

As our evening continued, I received wonderful homemade cards from Sarah, Drake, and

Vicki celebrating my second year back home and at Bailey's. Barb made a French apple pie that was so delicious, that I was the first to go for seconds. I was given that option as the celebrated guest of honor. Of course, I'm paying for that now, feeling similar to how full I felt on the morning after Thanksgiving.

Upon special request, Joel and Jessie were thrilled to drive past Bailey's before driving back home to get ready for bed. They were busy once more, pointing, smiling, giggling, and what looked like counting. We also took a quick detour on my desire to see George's Christmas display. It was grand, as it always is, but I did not see anything different compared to last year's display. George said that he might be ready to unveil his surprise by Friday. That was two days ago. Both Joel and Jessie have the powerful gift of observation. Neither of them saw any perceptible changes from last year. I hate to bug George again, but I think I may do that tomorrow after church.

Sunday, December 6, 2015, 5:53 p.m.

Every year, it's the same story. Almost everyone in Pilaf starts the football season excited about the Browns. I tried to temper my excitement this year, but they sucked me in after a couple of wins. Today, their loss to the red-hot Bengals made me jump off the Browns bandwagon. I need to stick to watching high school football. It's a shame the high school season ends on Thanksgiving Day.

I retraced my drive from bringing home the Christmas tree this afternoon and found absolutely no trace of the two-foot pine. My best guess is that someone found it and, at the very least, pulled it away from the side of the road. I'll have to find another one. Gracie will be asking me about it on Tuesday.

Church service was wonderful. There are some extra decorations around the sanctuary windows this year which made the snowscape look festive. The snow did not melt that much. The gray skies made all of the colorful decorations more vibrant. Pastor O'Connor's message about what Joseph and Mary may have been thinking leading up to the birth of Jesus was heartwarming. He spoke about it as though he had witnessed it himself. Indeed, we are all witnesses as we read the accounts in God's Word.

After Pastor O'Connor dismissed us, I saw Officer Caputo quietly talking to George. As I passed by, they glanced and gave me a friendly greeting, then continued talking about what seemed like the weather. I later met George as I headed out the door to warm up the car for my family. George said nothing about his decorations. If Officer Caputo told him about my extracurricular activities on his porch, he didn't mention it. I was going to ask him about his decorations, but decided to wait for a more appropriate time.

Monday, December 7, 2015, 8:49 a.m.

Jennifer was up before sunrise this morning. She woke me from a deep sleep, the kind when you are trying to figure out where you are, and what day of the week it is. To compound that, Jennifer asked me to check the front porch. There was a very large object on it and it concerned her. After orienting myself, I wandered down the stairs in my pajamas and saw that there was something blocking the normal view of the street. I had to get right up to the window to see that, indeed, there was a large object on the front porch. After trying to figure out what it was from the relative safety of the window, I gave up and grabbed a coat for a cautious look on the porch.

After slowly walking out of the front door, I watched for motion. There was none. The object was stationary. I motioned Jennifer to turn the porch light on. When she did, I saw a huge cardboard box that had a snug fit on the porch. Why was there a delivery being made before sunrise on a Monday? Then it struck me. The box looked familiar. I checked the shipping label and saw that it was actually shipped to George Kroeck. The box was actually empty. I started to laugh.

I returned inside and told Jennifer about my walk past George's house last week to see what was new on his Christmas display when I spotted a huge box on his porch. That's what Officer Caputo and George must have been planning when I saw them chatting so quietly after church yesterday.

After opening the store this morning, George walked in before his shift began at the post office. He had a mammoth smile that he could not conceal. He knew from my expression that I had seen his delivery with the help of Officer Caputo's truck. I could only say one thing as he came closer to the counter. I simply stood to my feet, clapping my hands, and saying, "Bravo! Well done!" A mug of coffee and a caramel apple muffin were my treat to

George for his creativity. I'll have to do the same for Officer Caputo if he comes in today.

It's quite a bit colder this morning. The snow from yesterday went from slushy to very, very crunchy during the overnight period. It feels like December.

Gracie has today off, so perhaps I can find a two-foot pine quickly before I get the third degree about not having a tree to decorate.

Monday, December 7, 2015, 4:44 p.m.

We are right in the middle of the earliest sunset period. Until next week, the sun sets a few minutes before 5 o'clock. Factor in the sun's angle at this time of year and add any amount of cloud cover, and what you get is a noticeably dark sky as early as 4 o'clock in the afternoon. I had to turn a few lights on some time ago. I need to get Joel and Drake to work with Gracie to put up a few more Christmas lights to make it cozy.

Uncle Ben popped in later than usual. He remembered that I was making mushroom bisque for the lunch crowd. A grilled cheese sandwich and mushroom bisque is what he ordered. It looked and smelled so good as I whipped it up that I made the same for myself and sat down with him at the counter. I was able to tell him that I was awaiting word from Stormy. (Little did I know that he would return my email only fifteen minutes after Uncle Ben left.) He then told me about finding a two-foot pine tree at the base of his porch steps on Saturday evening. He pulled it up onto his porch and thought it looked so grand that he started decorating it with lights and a few extra ornaments. I didn't have the heart to tell him that it was the tree I had lost. Now it all makes sense. That's where I swerved to miss a squirrel that dashed in front of my car. I must have been so focused on the squirrel, that I never noticed anything rolling off the roof. Looks like I'll need to find another suitable tree elsewhere.

Mr. Rayburn stopped by after school let out. I asked him about Mrs. Krumm. He said that she wasn't back in the classroom yet and had something that really laid her out. It was an odd bug that made her completely lose her appetite. The only thing that sounded remotely good to her was ginger ale and apple pie. Mr. Rayburn actually came in to see if I had any good cooking apples. He wanted to make her an apple pie. He did find enough of the variety that he was looking for to make one small pie. Perfect! That put a spring in his step and he was out the door before I could ask if I had seen him walking with Miss Miller about a week ago near the town gazebo. I suppose that it is just as well. It's really none of my business.

Joel and Jessie's whiteboard number is now up to 31. Whatever it is they are keeping track of, it's increasing more than one per day. I still haven't the foggiest idea what the significance of this number might be.

Tuesday, December 8, 2015, 8:55 a.m.

Stormy wants in. I knew that he would. Uncle Ben stopped by early this morning while it was still dark. I don't think he took two steps inside the front door before I told him that Stormy emailed back wanting to help Harry. Uncle Ben was all smiles. According to him, that news fueled his appetite. It must have! Not only did he have his usual cherry Danish, but asked for one of Maureen's cheese biscuits with a little fresh Ohio butter. We were safe discussing the next step since Harry was not coming to meet Uncle Ben today. I'll ask Stormy if he can come to Bailey's one week from today. That will give us enough time to iron out all the details and to see if Stormy has any ideas, too.

Speaking of Stormy, I just heard his weather segment on WPLF. I watched the very light snow that he was talking about falling outside the front window. It wasn't too cold this morning, but Stormy told us that the rest of the week would be quite chilly, but not too dreary.

I drove past George's place this morning on my way to the store. It's gorgeous, but there is virtually no change from last year as best as I can tell. All of the lights were on, but obviously there was no music from his speakers at that hour. George must not be having problems with sound this year, and I forgot to ask Uncle Ben if the two crows had made any appearances on or near his porch.

Gracie will be in before the lunch rush today. She promised to make her famous corn chowder. Once the word gets out, it's likely to be a busy lunch hour. That's good for me. I'm hoping she is so busy that she doesn't notice that I do not (yet) have her two-foot Christmas tree.

I discovered that I'm running a little low on Honeycrisp and Jonathan apples. That's not surprising with the heightened interest in apple pie this season. From what Donald Buckley tells me, both Jonathan and Honeycrisp are good apples for pie making. In fact, Donald likes to mix the two. I've heard many customers talking about blending more than one variety for that perfect pie. Jennifer makes one of the best, but I couldn't tell you what kind of apples she uses. I'll have to ask and set aside what she needs given this unusual run on apples.

Tuesday, December 8, 2015, 10:02 p.m.

Joel and Jessie are already fast asleep. I'm certain they're dreaming Christmas dreams. Earlier, they asked me if we could go for a car ride to look at Christmas displays after dinner tonight. How could I say no to such a sweet request that was full of Christmas spirit? I suggested going north toward Uncle Ben's house for a little variety, but I was met with immediate resistance. They wanted to drive down to Bailey's and back. They said there were more decorations to see between our home and Bailey's. Indeed, they were right. It was a lovely drive. Even though the light snow from earlier stopped in the afternoon, there was still enough on lawns and rooftops to give the rich colors of Christmas a magnificent glow. Joel and Jessie were in the back seat together bouncing from side-to-side. They also had scratch pads and pens in their hands. Every time we saw a display go by, they scribbled something on their scratch pads. I realized that the number I've been seeing may have something to do with our evening drives to look at all the decorations.

Once home, I sat in the den with Jennifer for a few minutes while the kids prepared for bedtime. After telling her about all the great decorations popping up everywhere, Joel and Jessie called us from upstairs. They were ready for bed and for our evening prayer together. It's always precious time. Tonight, we were in Jessie's room. After prayers were offered and Jessie was tucked in, I walked past the whiteboard and noticed a new number. Now it showed 42. I pointed to the number and asked if that was the number of houses that were decorated with Christmas lights between our home and Bailey's. Both Joel and Jessie were amazed with how I figured that out. However, they only counted houses that either had outdoor lights or candles in the window. An unlighted wreath, for instance, didn't count. On the flip side, Joel and Jessie would lobby each other to give bonus points for a very elaborate display. There was also something new above the number. It looked like a title: C L I P. Again, I pointed to this and took a wild guess: Christmas Lights In Pilaf? Bingo! I'm looking forward to seeing how large this number gets now.

While driving around in the car, I insisted on driving past George's house before coming home. I asked the kids to take a good look at his display to see if they could see anything new or different compared to last year. We all came up with the same conclusion. There was nothing new as far as we could tell. Why the big box on his porch? Its purpose could not have been empty bait for me. That's not the George I know. I don't get it.

Gracie made it in this morning with plenty of time to have the corn chowder ready for lunch. Don't ask me how word gets out so quickly, but it does. We were slammed for lunch. Every table and seat was taken and almost everyone had a cup of Gracie's corn chowder. The biggest surprise was who was eating together at the end of the counter closest to the front window. It was Mr. Rayburn and Miss Miller. It did not appear to be a coincidence since, at the end of their lunch, he brought a single check to the register to pay for their meal. For kicks, I asked them if they wanted any apple pie for dessert before they left. They passed, but Mr. Rayburn did say that they were actually talking about apple pie recipes while they enjoyed their corn chowder and sandwiches. Could Pilaf finally be witnessing a budding romance between two lovely people that we all knew would make a nice couple?

As busy as the lunch crows was, and as curious as we all were with who was sitting at the end of the counter for lunch, Gracie still managed to pull me aside to ask me where the two-foot Christmas tree was. I didn't have the heart to tell her that it was sitting on Uncle Ben's porch. I simply told her that I was still working on it.

Wednesday, December 9, 2015, 6:44 a.m.

It's a cold 18°F, but dry this morning. There are still plenty of places on the sidewalks and other walkways where the crusty snow remains and crunches underfoot. There are too many icy spots on Bailey's front porch. I hope to see the temperature rise enough above freezing to clear that off so customers have better footing. Today is also the first day where starting a fire in the woodstove moved from a desire for ambience to a necessity for my early morning customers and me.

Things have been so crazy-nutty in the last week, that I needed one of these quiet mornings to myself. I woke before my alarm and decided to head down to the store where I would make coffee and wait for my morning delivery from Giammalvo's Market. Between the furnace in the basement and the woodstove fire, Bailey's warmed up quickly. I guess I didn't realize how early I walked in the front door of the store. I was shocked when I glanced at the clock and saw that it was only 5:55 a.m. I paused to think of Dad and Mom. How I would love for them to experience this peaceful moment with me over a cup of coffee, studying God's Word.

It makes me think of Jesus' words to the woman at the well when He said that whoever drinks from the water that He serves will never thirst. Why, then, do I feel spiritually thirsty every so often? Perhaps it was the Lord speaking to me directly when I could hear Him telling me that I have to read His Word daily. Will, for instance, an eight ounce glass of water keep my body hydrated next week? Will a delightful breakfast today keep my body fueled for tomorrow afternoon? Of course not. How can I keep my spirit satisfied without feeding it daily with His Word? Not only is my body satisfied from this morning's oatmeal, but now my spirit is satisfied after spending time reading the Word that God gave to us.

It looks like a stable weather day ahead. I'll check Stormy's forecast coming on at 7:05 a.m. If it's as nice as I think it will be, I'll take a walk down the Jasmine Creek foot trail to see if I can find any decent looking two-foot pine trees to bring back for the store.

Wednesday, December 9, 2015, 8:12 p.m.

The kids tell me that Mrs. Krumm is still out, but that she will attempt to return tomorrow or Friday morning. I've missed her occasional visits with her eclectic assortment of checkout items. Even a year after understanding the strange array of purchases, I still have to chuckle to myself when she visits Bailey's. Even so, as has been the case from the beginning, we just don't ask.

Uncle Ben came in today to see if there was any additional word from Stormy. I've been checking my email all day, but so far Stormy hasn't responded to our suggested date of Tuesday. I'm sure his schedule is complicated by the fact that he has to juggle more than a dozen radio stations across Ohio and Indiana. I'm confident that we will make something work for everyone involved.

Uncle Ben had a large, pre-paid, flat-rate envelope that he handed me and asked me if I could drop that off at the post office by the final, daily 4:30 p.m. collection time. I was happy to, but I wondered why he could not drive over and drop it off himself if he needed it in today's mail. He appeared to be in a hurry and said that he needed to head to Borger, in the other direction, and wasn't sure if he could return in time. Sounded reasonable, although it did strike me as rather odd. I agreed and it set his mind at ease.

After he left, I could not help but notice that the return address was not actually from Uncle Ben. It was from Jimmy Giammalvo, and the address was that of Giammalvo's Market. The addressee was someone in Buffalo by the name of Mike Cejka. That name sounded so familiar, but I could not resolve much beyond that. Why would Uncle Ben have me put something in the mail from Giammalvo's Market? Perhaps he left in a hurry because he did not want to answer any probing questions.

George the mailman came in only minutes after Uncle Ben took off for Borger. Perfect! I figured that I could give the envelope to George and he could make sure it gets into the flow of outgoing mail. The first thing I asked him was about his Christmas decorations this year. I told him that our entire family determined that he had nothing new to show off this year. George responded by telling me that perhaps I was looking in the wrong place. I had no idea what he meant. I was in not in the mood for cerebral gymnastics, so I let the comment go. After getting him settled with an orange juice and English muffin, I showed him the envelope that Uncle Ben left me to mail. I asked him to take it in with him to work and to get it into the outbox. George looked at me like I was asking him to hold a tarantula. He flatly refused. But why? He scolded me and reminded me that, as a postal employee, he could not take someone else's mail outside the post office window while he was wearing his postal uniform. Really? I had never heard of such a policy before this.

Wanting to place it in the outbound box before the final collection time for the day, I left Gracie in charge when things slowed down after the lunch rush. It was cool, but sunny, so I walked down to the post office with the envelope. When I turned left on Minnetonka Street, my eyes immediately fell on a large, bubble-like object only feet from the steps leading up to the front doors of the post office. The bubble was huge and colorful. As I approached the post office, George's comments came to life. His new decorations were not at his house this year, but at the post office! The giant bubble had a lighted wintry scene inside with styrofoam snow whipping around inside. It was spectacular! George was giving me the business about postal rules. The task forced me to see his big Christmas surprise for all of Pilaf.

This is exactly the kind of stuff I missed in the big city. One would be hard-pressed to find an expression of anything related to Christmas at the library, post office, or city hall. The ACLU would have zero traction here. As friendly as everyone is in this town, they would be firmly and efficiently escorted outside the Pilaf boundaries.

With so much going on today, I failed to take my walk down the Jasmine Creek footpath. Maybe tomorrow.

Thursday, December 10, 2015, 7:53 a.m.

Mrs. Krumm walked through the front door of Bailey's this morning with as much energy as she had before she was confined to her home. It was almost as though her battle had never taken place. Uncle Ben and Mr. Rayburn were there as well. We all turned toward the door and stood to our feet, welcoming her with a big smiles. She mentioned that the one thing that prevented her energy levels from totally disappearing was apple pie. It started when she bought the last slice of apple pie in my pie case over a week ago. Apparently, once the word was out, many of Pilaf's best bakers went to work making and sending over apple pies. At one point, she said that there were five pies from five different bakers in her house. She pointed to Mr. Rayburn, since one of the pies came from him!

I was curious now. Which pie was the best one? I asked her, but Mrs. Krumm knows how to keep the peace between bakers. She said that they were all delicious and that each one had something delightfully unique about it. If Mrs. Krumm ran for mayor, she may just win with answers like that.

I told Joel and Jessie about the giant Christmas bubble at the Pilaf post office. They seemed excited about paying a visit. I promised that I would show them during tonight's Christmas light counting drive after dinner.

Still no word from Stormy, but I'm not concerned. I'm anxiously waiting to hear word about next Tuesday's plan of action.

Skies have turned dark once again, this time with light rain showers. The breeze is blowing moderately out of the southwest. With the porch thermometer boasting 49°F, all of the crunchy snow patches are gone. I've been thinking about purchasing a weather station that sends all of the weather information via radio transmitter. Only a decade ago, the only reliable home weather stations were wired, not to mention expensive. Cost has come down and the radio technology is amazing. I could place the monitor on the counter for customers. Pilafians talk an awful lot about the weather. Stormy would be proud.

I hope the rain quits. I plan on heading down the Jasmine Creek footpath in a few hours regardless of what the atmosphere is doing. I'd rather avoid a repeat of what happened when we browsed for our family Christmas tree.

Thursday, December 10, 2015, 9:01 p.m.

I was soaked, but Gracie was happy to see a little tree come through the front door of Bailey's. There must be something in the air that knows when I'm looking for a Christmas tree this year.

The Jasmine Creek footpath was dark, wet, and muddy. Fortunately, I had my hiking boots with me so at least this time, my feet remained relatively dry. For the longest time, nothing caught my eye. The trees were either too big or too scrappy looking. A crow landed about twenty yards ahead of me at one point. It looked like Bonnie or Clyde, one of the crows that caused so much mischief last Christmas. Since I wasn't finding anything that fit the bill, I suspended my search for a moment and followed the crow off the footpath. We ended up near the perfect little pine. It was getting squeezed out by two other larger pines on either side. It was clear that it would lose the battle for the space, so I brought it back to the store. It actually measured about twenty inches, shy of two feet. Unlike Charlie Brown's selection, this tree was full-bodied and would be able to handle as many ornaments and lights as Gracie put on it.

I heard from Stormy. He plans on arriving at Bailey's next Tuesday morning before his mid-morning radio feeds. He inquired about the speed of my WiFi to make sure that he was able to upload all of his feeds quickly. I assured him that my upload speed would be more than adequate. We may be a very quiet and deliberately-paced town, but we are well connected to the rest of the world. I'll tell Uncle Ben and we will start sketching out the details tomorrow morning.

During dinner, Joel and Jessie were visibly excited to tell me that Mrs. Krumm was back. What a delightful testimony to how well liked she is by the student body. I told them about her visit into the store and about all the apple pies she received. Jessie's eyes lit up. She told Jennifer that she should have made Mrs. Krumm her famous Mount Mansfield apple pie. If only she had known. My guess is that Mrs. Krumm would have given the blue ribbon to Jennifer. Am I biased? Indeed, I am, but with good reason.

After dinner, I drove Joel and Jessie on our Christmas light-counting mission between our home and Bailey's. The raindrops on our windows gave the neighborhood lights an interesting effect from inside the car. Granted, it was not as magical as fresh snow cover, but it was special in its own way.

Because there was little to no traffic on the road, I drove very slowly so that Joel and Jessie could enjoy their counting. After the task was done, I drove them past the Pilaf post office to see the giant Christmas globe. It was even more grand at night. In addition to the light that illuminated the inside of the bubble, George placed two LED spotlights on either side that slowly changed color. I asked Joel and Jessie if that was worth two points or more. They were quick to point out that, technically, it was not on the official route, but the display was so grand that they would add one point to tonight's CLIP number. Not until we were home did I see that the number was changed from 42 to 62. Christmas in Pilaf. Gotta love it.

Friday, December 11, 2015, 10:11 a.m.

I should have waited a day to find Bailey's tree. The sun is bright and much of the ground has dried out from yesterday's dreary rain. Oh, well. At least Gracie was pleased and is already placing a few ornaments on it so that it doesn't look barren. She is waiting until our lighting engineering team of Joel and Drake join the decorating fun tomorrow.

Uncle Ben arrived early this morning. Harry followed no more than a few minutes after him. They quickly sat down at their favorite table. Uncle Ben seemed to be eager to show Harry a couple of things in his Bible. I brought two mugs of coffee over as they looked up some passages in the book of Colossians. They didn't order anything to eat right away. I started busying myself restocking the apples that Donald brought me from his orchard. I didn't want to seem like I was being nosy. Once they were ready to order a few pastries, Uncle Ben waved me over. Right after they ordered, Uncle Ben smiled and told me that Harry was going to sit in on his Sunday morning study group before worship this week. Then he winked. Something was up. Harry was lukewarm on the idea of coming in an hour before worship until Uncle Ben told him that I had "volunteered" to make fig squares to bring to the study time. He winked again. In other words, I am now making fig squares for Sunday.

That's a very small price to pay for getting Harry into the Colossians study this Sunday ahead of our visit from Stormy. I never knew that Harry liked my fig squares. It has been almost two years since I made them. Naturally, I'm curious how Uncle Ben was able to connect so many dots. I'll have to ask him later since both he and Harry left the store together after a last cup of coffee.

Beyond the popular fig cookie brand found in supermarkets, there aren't too many desserts that use fig filling. I can thank my father for knowing where to get commercial-sized cans of fig paste. His fig squares were amazing! If my memory serves me right, my brother is the one who would special request Dad's fig squares whenever his birthday came around.

Friday, December 11, 2015, 5:00 p.m.

After an active day, the store is now quiet. The front porch lights went out a few minutes ago. The closed sign went up when I locked the door. I often wonder if the sign is even necessary since virtually everyone in Pilaf knows Bailey's hours. Somehow, it's a part of my routine that I can't seem to change. It's almost as though I need a reminder that Bailey's is closed. Without that step, I would likely linger, working on odds and ends that can be addressed tomorrow.

Skies were sunny all day. There was also a stunning sunset that filled the store with a deep salmon color before it faded. Even with clear skies, the deep twilight colors on the horizon cannot stop the winter dark from taking over within minutes after sunset. On the bright side, we are not dealing with several feet of windblown snow like we saw about a year ago.

George, Pilaf's amateur astronomer, came in after the lunch hour to remind me that the Geminid meteor shower will be peaking this weekend. He told me he saw a very bright meteor that zipped across the sky just before sunrise today. If the weather holds out, we won't be doing battle with hip-deep snow drifts. Last year's meteor show was wonderful, but I think the most memorable part was having to navigate the backyard after the blizzard. I'm sure that Joel and Jessie will be telling their kids about that when the next generation arrives.

Like an unusual super-conjunction of planets aligning, we had a rare gathering of apple connoisseurs by the fruit bin only a few hours ago. The sight took me by surprise. Donald Buckley, Mrs. Krumm, Mr. Rayburn, Miss Miller, and my Jennifer were all hovering near the apples. This super-conjunction of pie-makers was not a coincidence. As I worked my way toward them, I started to understand why this group was not anxious to shop anywhere else. They were all talking about the different varieties and combinations of apples that they used to make a great apple pie. Mr. Buckley stopped them all by insisting that Pilaf ought to have an apple pie baking contest. Everyone beamed at the thought of a blue ribbon hanging in their kitchen. I hated to throw a little cold water on the excitement, but their level of excitement went down noticeably after I reminded them that we would need a few judges that were completely non partisan. Mr. Buckley said he might have a solution, but offered no specifics.

Saturday, December 12, 2015, 10:23 a.m.

This seems to have been a season of contrasts. Since Thanksgiving, we have ping-ponged between bright, sunny, mild days, with days that have been dark, dreary, and cool or cold. There has been very little in between. It's back to thick, dark cloud cover this morning. It felt like the sun was struggling to let us all know that it was still there, somewhere above the layer of murky gray. The Bailey's porch thermometer indicated a rock-steady temperature of 32°F.

Days like this make me want to start a weather journal of some kind. I've tried in the past. My earliest one was when I was in middle school. It started as a class science project. I thought it was interesting and went beyond the single-week assignment since the weather pattern was active and it was winter. Then something happened. The weather became boring and stable. Taking the time to log a boring weather day wasn't much fun. String three or four of them along and my interest level dropped as fast as baseball-sized hail. When an active weather day came along, I wished I had been more vigilant at recording the boring days since they would have provided a kind of context that would have made the active weather even more exciting. I'd like to try again, perhaps starting on January 1. I'll have to consider getting a little more sophisticated, though. Somehow a casual glance at the porch thermometer seems to be an approach that is too informal.

 Uncle Ben stopped by with someone I've never met before. He was pleased to introduce me to Bruce Dilling, the mechanic who not only fixed Uncle Ben's car last year, but hosted him in a little cottage near his main house during the big blizzard. Bruce had some extra time to visit this weekend, and it seemed appropriate since the blizzard's arrival was exactly one year ago, or at least so I think it was. (I wish I had kept a weather journal to check these things.) Bruce is a tall and slender man with soft blue eyes. It was clear that he loves people. If you did not get along with Bruce, the problem is definately you. It was great meeting the mechanic that extended so much hospitality to a perfect stranger trying to get home. Bruce and his wife, Andrea, are staying with Uncle Ben tonight. They all promised to meet up with us again at church tomorrow morning. Not only will we have Bruce and his wife as guests, but Harry Buser, too.

On that note, I almost forgot to gather what I needed to make those fig squares today. Harry would have been disappointed with no fig squares to munch on before the Bible study time. Thank goodness I keep a couple of cans of fig paste in the back.

Joel and Drake are here today while the girls head into the city. They left from the store after dropping off the boys. That was an hour ago. Similar to last year, the boys are assessing what needs to be done in the store in terms of Christmas decorations. They are working with Gracie to make the two-foot Christmas tree look like the best Christmas tree in Pilaf.

Saturday, December 12, 2015, 5:52 p.m.

Where did today go? Typically, the time crunch we all feel during the workweek tends to expand and relax, at least a little, on Saturday. Not today, and it certainly wasn't the weather. If anything, the dark gloominess of the day made time seem to pass more slowly. I'm sure it was the added pressure of ensuring the fig squares were done, and that they were at least palatable. It has been a little while since I've made these jewels. The last thing I want is for Harry to come into the room we use for our Sunday morning group study, grab a fig square that tasted sub-par, and find a way to maneuver his way to the back door. Much of my afternoon was spent on making sure that the crust was buttery and flakey, a process that takes time. After the squares came out of the oven, I decided to crown them with a vanilla-butter icing. That always produced rave reviews, but again, you can't rush through the process. In the end, I am convinced that people will stop talking about apple pie for a little while.

In between the baking steps, I took a break from the back kitchen to check in on Gracie, Joel, and Drake. After seeing the joy on everyone's faces as they decorated the small Christmas tree, I wanted to drop everything I was doing and find a quiet place at the counter just to watch the process unfold. Alas, I had to be satisfied with the few brief glimpses of this scene that the fig squares would afford.

About thirty minutes before closing, I wandered out of the kitchen and saw Gracie, Joel, and Drake, joined by George and Uncle Ben, sitting at the counter with hot chocolate, looking at the finished decorating job. I could hardly believe my own eyes. Was that the little scrappy pine that I pulled out of the woods near the Jasmine Creek? It was as if I witnessed a real-life version of what happened when the Charlie Brown cartoon gang fixed up that little emaciated tree. I understood why everyone was looking so jubilant. After seeing the transformed tree, I insisted that Gracie make complimentary hot chocolate for everyone in the store.

It was high time to leave the Christmas lights on in the store round-the-clock. Nowadays, with cool-burning LED lights, there is no concern of lights overheating unlike when Frank Bailey owned the store. It add ambience to Pilaf. The real test will come later tonight when I drive Joel and Jessie back to the store for the Christmas light count. I'm sure that, at the very least, we will earn one point. Will there be a bonus point because they were involved in this display? I would not argue if they gave themselves a hundred extra points! It was magnificent.

The girls are not home yet from the city. It's dark, and a rain and snow mixture has started to fall. I'm hoping they will be home soon. I'm not fond of anyone I know driving when the weather starts getting slippery.

I promised everyone a tasty, but simple dinner tonight. I'm certain there will be no complaints about bringing home some of Gracie's corn chowder as a side to the burgers I'm about to pan fry.

Car doors! The girls are back. After a day of running around, making dinner and hearing all about their day will be a piece of cake compared to the fussiness of fig squares.

Sunday, December 13, 2015, 7:00 a.m.

Last night's sleep was phenomenally recharging. I woke before the alarm so refreshed that it felt like I woke up on a tropical island without a single care in the world. The only problem was the visual conflict of looking out the sliding glass door and seeing plenty of light reflecting off the snow that fell overnight. Why is it that the white sands of any tropical coast don't reflect artificial light like a fresh blanket of Ohio snow? I wonder if people living on lush, tropical islands ever dream of a white Christmas as a coveted surrounding? I don't know anyone who is a permanent resident on a tropical island, otherwise I would ask.

I have not been greeted by Sammy this morning. That's a bit unusual. He may be curled up in a warm, tight little ball in a small space to stay warm. The kitchen floor seems colder than usual and my fleece jacket is just barely adequate. I checked the thermometer at the kitchen window and saw that we dropped down to 9°F, a rather dramatic drop from just a few days ago. Only then did I recall hearing the constant whirring of the heating fans since my eyes opened.

The coffee was particularly tasty this morning. I'm sure it's the chill in the air. Admittedly, there is something cozy about watching Pilaf come to life surrounded by the pre-dawn sky and a fresh snowfall. I was only a little tempted to turn on the deck light to see how much snow we received, but thought that doing so would ruin the peaceful moment. I'll guess two inches and let the dawn light slowly reveal how close I am.

The fig squares meticulously arranged inside the glass cake stand and cover is something pleasing to the eye. I wish I could have one now. They would taste wonderful with this mug of coffee. Upon closer examination, it looked like one was missing from the top row. Either that, or I was so tired yesterday when I arranged them, that their placement wasn't as meticulous as I thought. I decided to rearrange the top row knowing that I might disturb the icing on the second layer from the top. It took a few minutes, but I did get the job done without making a mess of the next row. Still, it bothers me that I would have done such a shoddy job on the top row. I should have counted the squares yesterday. I could do some quick math for divisible numbers, but I would need a second cup of coffee to even try to count this mound since some of the squares are not visible. Maybe later. Maybe not.

The peak of this year's Geminids did not get an audience in Pilaf. Last night's cloud cover, rain, and snow kept us all indoors. It's just as well. After a long day of activities for everyone, we all needed to turn in early. I'm sure that George was disappointed.

Sunday, December 13, 2015, 4:47 p.m.

Why is it that some of us have favorite numbers? Is it the shape of the number? Is it the amount that the number represents? There certainly is a Biblical significance in numbers, seven being the number of perfection and completion for example. I say that because, for some odd reason I cannot explain, I like virtually any combination of the numbers 4 and 7 together. Note the time above.

I like 4:47 p.m., especially in the winter months. The Christmas lights are starting to glow, skies are trending toward twilight, and Pilafians are cozying in for an evening meal with family. 4:47 p.m. doesn't have the same significance in the summer, though. Perhaps it's too bright, too sunny, or too warm. That's when 77 becomes my favorite number. In my humble opinion, it's the perfect afternoon summer temperature when the sun is out and the humidity is low. Naturally, that temperature is in Fahrenheit, not Celsius. 77°C would be problematic.

The arctic chill meant a new assortment of winter attire showing up at church today. Jennifer was somewhat anxious to sport a new furry hat that she picked up in the city yesterday. Not only was it functionally warm (#1 in my book), but it was fashionably avant garde (#1 in Jennifer's book). Function vs. fashion. It's one of those guy-girl things.

We all arrived early, well before the Sunday morning study group. Those in the study group that arrived before me ooooo'd and ahhhhh'd at the display of fig squares inside the glass cake stand. I told everyone that they had to wait for Harry. I was saving the first square for him. The longer we waited, the more I wondered if Harry was going to bail out on us. Finally, at 9:28 a.m., Harry walked in, but he was not looking for the fig squares as I anticipated. Instead, he was quite shaken up. Few of us could understand what he was trying to say.

Eventually, in between gasps for air, we were able to catch enough of his story. He almost went off the road on the way to church. He could not understand how he did not end up in the culvert near Potter's corn and soybean field. Surrounding Harry with reassurance and gratefulness that he was unharmed was much more important than starting our study on time. We gave Harry a few moments to rest, and after about fifteen minutes, he asked if we could begin.

After we all took our seats, Jennifer walked over to Harry and offered him a mug of coffee and one of my fig squares. Suddenly, the world regained its rosy color. Much to Uncle Ben's credit, he kept the study short and focused, staying on Colossians 1:15. We all spent a great deal of time talking about how Jesus is the visible image of the invisible God. Harry watched everyone intently. While he did not say much, you could see that his light bulbs were coming on. Uncle Ben saw this happening, too. He wrapped up the study early to let Harry enjoy both the revelation and another fig square.

Following the worship service, Officer Caputo pulled Harry aside and asked him more about his close call with the culvert since he passed a set of tracks in the snow that seemed to defy logic. Uncle Ben and I joined the conversation just as Officer Caputo asked Harry if he would show him the place where his car had briefly spun out of control. They invited us to come along. Jennifer and the kids took the car home and I joined Harry, Officer Caputo, and Uncle Ben.

When we arrived at the place where Harry lost control of the car, the rear tire skid tracks were still clearly visible. They skidded to the right while the car had spun counter-clockwise. The tire tracks ended at the edge of the road. The tire tracks came back onto the road about thirty yards from where they seemed to vanish. His car should have tipped backward into the culvert, several feet deep. Harry was incredulous. He claimed that he never felt anything that would indicate his car would slip into the culvert. Because he knew the road so well, he anticipated the short drop. Instead, his car regained traction and seemed to correct itself back onto the road and in his own lane. It was as though there was some kind of road extension preventing Harry's car from slipping down into the culvert, yet there was absolutely no evidence of it. Without any traffic coming by for several minutes, we were all quiet, trying to make sense of this event. Harry finally looked at us with a nervous smile and said: "Visible image of the invisible God."

Monday, December 14, 2015, 8:42 a.m.

Pilaf's deep chill continues. My drive to Bailey's was extra cautious given Harry's Sunday morning incident. Anyone watching out their window as I drove by might have wondered why my speed was so slow. Perhaps I incited alarm at the thought there was a new layer of snow or ice and the road.

Joel and Jessie's C.L.I.P. number has enjoyed another surge since late last week. I made certain that their quilts were covering them before leaving for the store and noticed that the number is now 71. I'm now wondering if we will see that number rise to 100 by Christmas Eve. I never really thought about counting the number of displays I see at Christmas between our home and Bailey's. I just enjoy the show. I'm paying a bit more attention this year.

Uncle Ben was in very early today, at 6:30 a.m. In light of yesterday's events, he was visibly eager about Stormy's visit tomorrow morning. Harry was starting to grasp the reality of Jesus in ways that were once far from his understanding.

Harry will meet Uncle Ben at 8:30 a.m. tomorrow. They will sit at their favorite table by the front window. Stormy will have already arrived and will be seated at another table close enough so that they will be able to hear Stormy begin feeding his radio forecasts between 8:45 a.m. and the top of the 9 o'clock hour. The store should be sufficiently quiet by then.

Before Uncle Ben left the store, we paused for a few minutes to pray that all would go well and that Harry would receive a revelation.

Monday, December 14, 2015, 5:06 p.m.

It seems like Pilaf has forgotten about apples, at least for the moment. Word has spread about the fig squares that I brought to the Sunday morning study group at church. Even Miss Miller came in at lunch wondering if there were any fig squares available. Remarkably, there were two left after I retrieved the dish from the adult classroom. I brought them back to the store and placed them in the back of the pastry counter. Uncle Ben spotted them both earlier this morning and laid claim to one of them with his coffee while we mapped out tomorrow's visit from Stormy. Since I'd really like to try Miss Miller's pie this Christmas, I gladly gave her the remaining square in hopes that she will return the favor at apple pie time.

I received an email from Stormy just after lunchtime confirming that he would arrive shortly before 8 o'clock to set up his portable laptop so that he could quietly prepare before recording and feeding his radio forecasts to his client stations. The only thing that I wonder about is Stormy's presence itself. Can Uncle Ben keep Harry focused enough on their morning study that Harry will pay no attention to an unfamiliar guest with a laptop across the room? We shall see.

Jimmy Giammalvo stopped by during the mid-afternoon. School had let out, so Mr. Rayburn and Mrs. Krumm were there when Jimmy placed a box on the counter and told everyone to gather around. As he opened the box, we saw a colorful array of what looked like candy sticks of some sort. The Linakers from Fleetwood in the U.K. sent a box of something called Blackpool rock, a kind of candy stick that is very popular with tourists visiting the seaside destination near their hometown. They looked like Christmas candy canes without the hook, but one bite is all it took to convince me that these were far different (and far better, in my humble opinion!). The texture was nowhere near as hard as a candy cane, but hard enough to have to bite down into the stick in order to break a piece off. Once in the mouth, it became very chewable. That's when the explosion of flavors were released. Everyone who was in the store had the chance to try some. It was thoughtful of the Linakers to send the goody box, and just as kind that Jimmy brought the box over to share with us at the store. Before he left, Jimmy pulled out a green-apple flavored stick and asked me to take it home to Jennifer. I wish there was a way to send them a box of fig squares from Pilaf!

It has been a quiet weather day. After a cold and gray start, we finally saw the sun break through just before the lunch rush. I hope the weather stays quiet tonight and tomorrow. I wouldn't want anything to prevent Stormy from joining us.

Tuesday, December 15, 2015, 5:22 a.m.

I thought I had outgrown this kind of thing by now. I went to bed last night thinking about how everything might come together today, and I could not fall asleep. I think I finally fell asleep, but the operative word here is "think." That's because when I wasn't awake thinking about "Operation Stormy," I was dreaming about being at Bailey's, getting things ready. It all felt strangely seamless. I finally stopped fighting it and got out of bed about twenty minutes ago.

I just looked out the window. My body gave me a surge of adrenalin that would insure that sleep would not return to my eyes this morning. That's because my eyes were busy processing what looked like new snowfall. A flick of the back deck light confirmed my worst suspicion. There was only an inch or two, but it was still snowing.

As a kid, I would loved a morning like this. Joel and Jessie are going to be thrilled. I wish I could join their anticipated delight. I doubt there is enough to cancel school today, but my confidence has been challenged many times in recent years.

In an attempt to regain my meteorological composure, I fired up the coffee maker. I could sure use some of Uncle Ben's gortons right now. Second choice would have been a fig square.

Tuesday, December 15, 2015, 3:57 p.m.

Tired is an understatement. The more I walk through this day, the more I think that sleep was something that fled from me at every toss and turn last night. As busy as Bailey's was today, there isn't a single soul that remains except me. Gracie went home at 2 o'clock. George was my most recent and final customer. He left almost thirty minutes ago. I'm sure the quiet is amplifying my desire for a good night's sleep. If no one else swings by between now and 4:30 p.m., I'll call it a day and look forward to smelling Jennifer's tuna casserole, or a long nap. Both options have strong appeal.

The morning snowfall thankfully ended as I drove to the store. The roads were not as slippery as I had envisioned. Fears of Stormy getting stuck or delayed were a product of my imagination. Even so, I was relieved when Stormy walked into Bailey's just before 8 o'clock. After giving him a warm welcome and a quick tour of Bailey's, I showed him to his table and brought him a mug of fresh coffee and one of the fig squares from a new, small batch I made yesterday. Stormy set up his laptop computer and portable audio gear and went to work, but not before pausing to ask me about the fig squares. He really liked them and wondered how often I carried them. When I told him that I made a small batch yesterday, he immediately asked me to save one so that he could take it home to his wife, a culinary artist in her own right.

Before Uncle Ben and Harry Buser arrived, Stormy had one early feed to record for WXRF-FM in Bolivar. His voice carried through the store. Why should I have expected anything different? He is a professional in the media. There was no possibility that Harry will be able to ignore Stormy's unique signature voice only a few tables away.

Uncle Ben and Harry arrived right on time at 8:30 a.m. I immediately attended to their needs since I did not want Harry to be distracted with someone "new" across the room. There was no need to be concerned. The minute I gave him a fig square and a cup of coffee, he was focused on enjoying something he wasn't expecting. Uncle Ben opened up his Bible to Colossians chapter one and they began going over it again. Neither of them said anything about the guy on his laptop computer on the other side of the store. In fact, when I refreshed Harry's coffee, he asked if I had heard Stormy's forecast on WPLF this morning. I must admit, his question threw me.

At exactly 8:50 a.m., Stormy put on his headphones, adjusted his portable microphone, and waited for an introduction that only he would hear from the morning DJ on WPLF. Then his voice boomed out and found every nook and cranny of the store as he talked about the morning snow we had.

Harry stopped to listen. He thought that he was hearing a radio that I had turned up until he realized the voice was coming from a real person. The only other person that it could be was the stranger in the corner with headphones on his head. When Stormy was done, Harry was dumbfounded to discover that the meteorologist that he listens to every morning was sitting only feet away. Stormy went over and introduced himself.

Uncle Ben explained that the voice Harry heard on the radio actually belonged to a real person, even though none of us ever saw Stormy in person during any weather segment. That did not mean that he didn't exist. Uncle Ben quoted more Scripture about when Jesus told His disciples that His sheep know His voice, even if they don't see him. The sheep recognize His voice just as we are to recognize Jesus' voice even if we don't yet see him eye-to-eye. That will happen someday.

All the bells and whistles sounded for Harry. Between the tire tracks that went to nowhere and Stormy's live radio feed inside Bailey's, he suddenly felt close to a heavenly Father that seemed more real to him than the table he was using. Stormy was glad to have participated in bringing this Scripture to life for a fellow believer on this journey of faith. Harry was so excited that everyone would go to such an extraordinary measure to help him grab onto a great, spiritual truth. Harry has a new sparkle in his eye and a spring in his step today. How fun to witness such a moment.

Wednesday, December 16, 2015, 9:15 a.m.

Last night's sleep was long, refreshing, and satisfying in every way. I don't think it would have been so sweet had I taken that pre-dinner nap after I drove home. For starters, I probably wouldn't have wanted to wake up after thirty or sixty minutes. Jessie pointed to a spot on our Christmas tree that was not very well lit. All of the lights were functioning just fine, but it appeared as though we might have been a little careless in placing the lights on the tree. I took the task as a way to stay awake and engaged with my family.

Sammy seemed a little nervous when I got on my knees, then on my side right next to the lowest branches of the tree. Once I started sliding under the tree, Sammy scrambled and left the room. Does he really still remember what happened to him last year?

I found a comfortable place under the tree and adjusted the lights so that the lower, left side was not as dark. Unfortunately, Jessie left the living room so I could not ask her if it looked better. Before shuffling out from underneath the tree, I stared up from the bottom and admired all the lights and ornaments. It was a truly unique perspective, and in my case, spellbinding. I was so comfortable that I closed my eyes for just a moment. That was a mistake. My body took what must have been only seconds to fall into a deep sleep.

My very next conscious moment was when Sammy pounced on my lower stomach which made me want to sit up quickly. Unfortunately, having just fallen asleep, I was completely disoriented. In my confusion, I pushed up against the bottom of the Christmas tree. It ceremoniously began its gravity assisted journey to our living room floor. Sammy's eyes were wide with sudden fear. He escaped the falling tree by a cat tail's width. Jennifer and Jessie came rushing in. They wanted to laugh, but they didn't. This is getting to be an annual tradition.

Wednesday, December 16, 2015, 7:56 p.m.

Jennifer brought the kids by the store after school this afternoon. One week from now, their Christmas break will have already begun but you might have thought that it already started. I so love Christmas in Pilaf.

Despite their general excitement over Christmas, they seemed concerned over George's post office snow globe. They said that it looked "sad." After asking a few questions, it sounds like the globe is a bit deflated. The New England Patriots are not in Ohio playing the Browns this weekend, so perhaps we can rule out foul play. It's probably a simple matter of a failing air pump. After closing up Bailey's for the night, I made it a point to drive by the post office to check on things. George's globe looked far more deflated than Joel and Jessie had described.

I called George to alert him about his half-imploded Christmas bubble. I was not the first one to call him. He received several calls from late-shifters at the post office, as well as Officer Caputo. I asked him if he wanted a side-kick to check things out. Besides, Joel has a new, high-output LED flashlight that he wanted to try out on a real-life situation. Since we are all done with dinner, and since all of the after-dinner chores were done, the whole family wanted to go. George will be looking for me in ten minutes.

Thursday, December 17, 2015, 8:01 a.m.

Uncle Ben arrived early this morning. He brought what was left of a small container of gortons that he made last week, enough for two English muffins. He certainly has mastered the art of making them over the past year. I've not had to go any more than a few months without sampling a new batch. Each one gets better and better (not to say there was anything wrong with the first batch).

He had not yet heard about Pilaf's Christmas Globe Deflategate. I filled him in on how George and I drove back to the post office last evening. The globe was almost completely deflated by the time we examined it closely. The pump was still running at full speed. The problem was not the pump. This is where Joel's new flashlight came in very handy. As we carefully circled the globe, Joel noticed a tear in the plastic on the right, bottom side. Upon closer examination, it looked like a deliberate puncture. Who would do such a thing, and why? George asked Joel to illuminate the inside of the globe. Something didn't look right. Sure enough, one of the plastic candy canes inside the globe scene was missing. Outrage! None of us has ever seen anything vandalized in Pilaf before today. George scheduled a meeting with Officer Caputo to file an incident report later today.

I was listening to Gary Bittner on WPLF-FM earlier this morning. He was interviewing Donald Buckley about this year's apple crop. Somehow, Gary steered the conversation to apple pies and how his wife made the best one around. Donald admitted that he had heard that from far too many people in Pilaf and that soon, he would announce something very big happening in our wonderful, cozy town. Could this be an apple pie baking contest? I'd like to volunteer as a judge!

Thursday, December 17, 2015, 5:11 p.m.

Jimmy Giammalvo stopped in for ten minutes before I closed the store tonight. It was good to catch up since both of us get somewhat busy during the Christmas season. He saw my brother Jim in the store earlier and suggested we all get together for a new board game that he and Alice picked up during his trip to Iceland a few months ago. Jim immediately suggested tomorrow night before we all became too busy with other Christmas plans and preparations. I don't think we have anything on the calendar for tomorrow night. I'll check with Jennifer.

George came in after his route was done today. I haven't seen George so frustrated since Mrs. Sauerkraut mailbox gave him such a fit last Christmas. He said he did manage to fix the globe on his lunch break with materials he purchased, namely duct tape. The tape was plenty strong to hold everything together and to keep the globe inflated. Even though the duct tape job was invisible to the passer-by, it was hard to ignore the fact that a figurine inside the globe was supposed to be holding something that wasn't in his hand. That little elf in the fuzzy hat and green tights was missing his candy cane.

Friday, December 18, 2015, 9:05 a.m.

The kids could hardly get into the bedtime routine last evening. Today would truly be their last day of serious schoolwork before the classrooms turn into nearly continuous Christmas celebrations next Monday and Tuesday morning. Both Joel and Jessie have tests for which they've been studying, so they have been pretty quiet for the last few evenings. The cork pops off tonight, I'm sure. The thought makes me smile. I love every second of it.

Joel and Jessie's C.L.I.P. number actually went down for some reason. I noticed the number on each of their boards this morning when I checked their covers before heading to the store. The number went down from 83 on Wednesday to 82 sometime last night before they went to bed. Is that even possible in Pilaf? As tempted as I was to wake them before I left for Bailey's, I'll have to be satisfied with asking them about it when I get home tonight.

We've not seen many opportunities for snowfall so far this December. It certainly does not dampen the Christmas spirit in this town though. What the snowfall does offer is a kind of enhancement to the nighttime lights that adorn virtually every nook and cranny. Last year's mid-December blizzard covered Pilaf with snow to some degree right through to the New Year. The snowfall has been sporadic and inconsistent this year. The ground is bare once more and the sun is shining with the same kind of confidence that it has in early November. Stormy's forecast this morning isn't particularly encouraging to our kids who remember how snowy it was last December. Because our weather memories are generally short, most of our youth tend to think that December brings a cornucopia of snow every year. I like the one and two-inch snowfalls we have seen thus far. While it does mean that we have to drive with a winter mindset, at least it isn't crippling to our daily routines.

Gracie has the day off today. In fact, she is off until Monday. I develop a new appreciation for her when she takes more than a day off. When she was gone for a week last August, it took her more than a week to get us back on track with all of the little things she does that are not a part of my routine. I'll make certain that she doesn't go through that on Monday. It will probably mean a later close on Saturday, but I'd rather stay here at Bailey's until midnight than return to my routine in the city. I've not forgotten the Divine blessing that brought me here.

Friday, December 18, 2015, 5:43 p.m.

This is getting ridiculous. George came in about an hour ago to tell me that the mystery vandal was at it again, this time striking in broad daylight. Since I did not have the liberty of leaving Bailey's before nightfall, I had to be satisfied with the picture

that George painted with a short chronology of
events and discovery of the offense.

When George stepped out of the post office
around 2 o'clock, all was well. The giant snow globe
was fully inflated minus one candy cane. I think
everyone became used to seeing the elf seemingly
holding an imaginary object. George was on his way
to Mrs. Sauerkraut's house to pick up a Christmas
package that she needed to mail. (Leave it to a spry
88-year-old woman to learn how to open an online
postal account, print a postage-paid label, and
request a package to be picked up.) Since the day
was pleasant and his other duties were completed,
George walked to Mrs. Sauerkraut's home, only ten
minutes away. After picking up the package, George
returned to the post office and was surprised to see
the globe deflated again. At first, he thought perhaps
the duct tape had come loose, but the surprise
turned to exasperation when he saw that the duct
tape was still intact and that a second puncture was
made only inches away from the first one. After
another careful inventory of the contents of the
globe, this time the house inside the globe was also
deflated. That was because the chimney was
somehow hacked off. George said that no one near
the post office saw anything suspicious. Whoever did
this was brazen enough to do it in broad daylight.

This made me angry. Who in their right
mind would cause senseless vandalism to a beloved
Christmas gift to Pilaf from a man who has no

enemies? Officer Caputo met George just as I was about to close the store. As I closed up shop, I let the two use the counter to try to come up with a way to catch the scoundrel. George recalled that Neil Manausa, his neighbor, had that high-tech surveillance system that he might be able to borrow for a day or two. Neil was very upset after hearing about the first vandalism incident, so they were certain that he would do anything to help stop this bah-humbug nonsense. While George and Officer Caputo left the store with a plan, I am preparing to leave the store with an appetite. We are headed to Jim and Barb's for a fun, no-fuss dinner, and some family fun. I'll refuse to allow a local grinch to spoil what promises to be a great evening.

Saturday, December 19, 2015, 7:12 a.m.

I drove past the post office on the way in to Bailey's this morning and the giant snow globe was looking good again. Armed with duct tape, George must have taped the globe's chimney gap, because the house was inflated along with the globe portion as well. I wasn't able to determine whether or not there was a surveillance system in place to catch the hooligan, but I'm confident that something is in place. I won't get too close for fear of any camera recording me checking on the globe. I think I've learned my lesson from trying to innocently look around on George's porch.

Joel and Jessie briefed me on the C.L.I.P. number's reduction yesterday. I was thinking far too much about complex scenarios. The explanation was rather simple. When Joel and Jessie piled into the car in order to take an inventory of Christmas lights, something did look odd, but I could not place my finger on it. Because the official C.L.I.P. number begins at our house and ends at Bailey's, the number went down one because I did not turn on our own Christmas lights yet. I like doing it the old-fashioned way, and that is, flicking a switch. It's as though I am personally adding Christmas spirit to the neighborhood and passers-by. It gives me pause to smile almost every time. I take careful account of the sights, sounds, and smell of our home as I'm turning on the lights. Many times, the kids are filling the house with playful holiday sounds. There are moments when the scent of gingerbread cookies fill the house. There are still other times when the yellow glow of the dinner table candles cast a sense of peace around the dining room. It's all good, very good. Sometime next week, I'll leave the Christmas decorations on around the clock until at least the day after Christmas. This year, I'll likely leave them on through December 27th simply because it falls on a Sunday.

We had a great evening at Jim and Barb's house. I still marvel at their little pine tree at the entrance of their driveway. I could stare at its new, color-changing LED lights while listening to Christmas tunes on my smartphone for hours. Drake apparently programmed it to do other things, too, but everyone seems to like the slow color fades the most.

Jimmy and Alice Giammalvo were there, as was Uncle Ben. The meal was simple, but special. We had hot dogs, but not just any hot dog. These premium, all-beef, uncured hot dogs come from the same place that supplies the top-of-the-line steaks to world class restaurants around the United States. Jimmy explained that he wanted to go the extra mile with an end in mind. What he did not tell anyone until the hot dogs were being steamed was that he brought a condiment with him. Not just any condiment, but the one from that little hot dog stand that he was able to find when he revisited Reykjavik, Iceland a few months ago. The container was very unassuming, but Jimmy guaranteed that its content was not. Jimmy wasn't joking. Between the delightful snap of the casing on the premium hot dogs and the condiment from the hot dog stand in Iceland, all but one hot dog remained in the end. Only the kids had enough room for dessert.

In keeping with the Icelandic theme, Jimmy pulled out the board game they brought back from their trip to the arctic island nation. It's called Krokur. I thought it was just a random, fun-to-say, and easy-to-remember name for this unique game. Jimmy told us that Krokur is the Icelandic word for detour. Out of curiosity, Drake looked it up on a translation application on his smart tablet, confirming it. Judging from how the game is played, there is a strategy involved using a series of directional arrows to try to force your opponent away from his destination, while trying to get to yours. None of us had ever played anything like this. It was easy to learn, and very fun to play. Uncle Ben claimed that he had never seen the game before, but he sure cleaned our clocks all night. Beginners luck?

Saturday, December 19, 2015, 6:12 p.m.

The day started on a quiet note. That changed after hearing Donald Buckley interviewed on our local radio station, WPLF. He was taking questions about fruit crops in general, but a lot of the focus was on what to do with this year's abundance of apples. The chatter about the types of apples, and recipes for applesauce and such was all very interesting. But then my ears perked up when he said that he was going to make an important announcement for anyone who liked making apple pies. He would be making this announcement after church on Sunday afternoon in the community dining hall where the Christmas card exchange table is set up. Could this be the apple pie baking contest taking shape?

I guess I did not realize how popular our local radio station was with everyone in our little town. As time went by and as people wandered in for a bite to eat or to pick up a few items for the weekend, it seemed everyone had heard the interview. I'm certain that's why we seemed to have an unusual "people jam" by the produce today. There were a few customers that came up to the cash register with a few apples, but I noticed a lot of chatter and what looked like careful scrutiny over the apples that were on display. I hope people start buying them instead of picking up nearly every single one and placing it back.

George stopped by before heading home. He walked past the giant snow globe. Aside from the missing candy cane and house chimney, everything looked normal. George's neighbor, Neil, did set up an elaborate surveillance system at the post office as I suspected. Perhaps now that the word is out that the globe is under constant surveillance, the vandal won't return. We have enough going on with a possible pie-baking contest.

It was a long, but satisfying day here at the store. Nonetheless, I know that Gracie is not here by looking at the clock. I'm still not quite done cleaning up before I can lock the door behind me until Monday morning. Gracie would have had everything done long ago. At least the weather was sunny, cool, and dry. I might have been kept here much later on a day when customers are tracking in snow, mud, and salt.

Another benefit of the quiet, dry weather has been seeing the late afternoon moon grow from a crescent to nearly half full tonight. I actually caught several glimpses of it in the south window by my office in the back. What a great timepiece in the sky. The heavens really do declare the glory of our heavenly Father!

Sunday, December 20, 2015, 7:00 a.m.

I wonder what cats think about when they see snow falling. They seem genuinely excited, almost as though they were tracking a rodent.

Perhaps the exercise keeps them in practice for chasing live things. Whatever the reason, Sammy is focused, looking out the back deck sliding glass door with his tail waving back and forth with precision. I was surprised to find the snow this morning after seeing such a clear, bright, beautiful gibbous moon last night during my trek home.

For the second consecutive Sunday, there is snow to contend with for the drive to church. I'm certain of two things as I watch the flakes falling. The first is that Harry will consider staying put, not wanting to repeat the scenario from last week. The second is that he will make the decision to brave the elements. I sense that he is enjoying his new spiritual breakthrough and does not want the momentum to stop. Seeing that kind of zeal does wonders for my own faith walk. God knew that he was going to help more than one man when Harry clung to and understood a Scripture passage that once left him confused at best.

Joel and Jessie asked me to escort them on a C.L.I.P. run last night. It was a bit later than our usual drive since Jennifer planned dinner a little late with Gracie out of town. It was 9:30 p.m. when we took our Christmas light run, so there was little chance of it being short one. Our outdoor lights were already on when I arrived home. It had been dark for almost two hours, so I certainly didn't mind. In fact, it was a fun way to see our handiwork from a passer-by perspective. I loved what I saw.

After our drive, the C.L.I.P. number was recorded and displayed at 99. At this late stage, I have to wonder if there are any hold-outs that would push that number to 100. I suppose there is still a chance since I was surprised to see the number increase as much as it did in the last seven days. Joel and Jessie seem to think that it will.

Jennifer is filling the kitchen with the aroma of duck bacon sizzling in the fry pan, a special treat. I can tell the difference between the aroma of regular pork bacon and duck bacon in the frying pan. To me, it smells like Christmas or Easter, since Jennifer always hunts it down for it for those cozy holiday mornings. It won't be long before the aroma will wake Joel and Jessie from their slumber. I hope they will have good memories when they are adults and on their own when they smell bacon frying in their own homes.

Sunday, December 20, 2015, 4:42 p.m.

The snow stopped as soon as the first piece of duck bacon was pulled off the serving plate this morning. There did not appear to be much accumulation. As the morning light revealed the landscape, blades of grass were still visible above a thin coating of very wet snow. It was unlike me not to check on the temperature after grabbing a cup of coffee. I suppose that I was enjoying the conversation with my bride too much to think about it. After breakfast, I saw that more of the lawn was showing. That's when I checked the thermometer just outside the kitchen window. It was not as cold as it looked at 36°F.

Jennifer had me hang the thermometer there when we moved in only a couple of years ago. She did not have one at our place in the city and always asked me to install one for her. It's something she just liked knowing. She said it would help her make decisions on how to dress the kids in the morning. I never did hang one though. I was always too swamped with work from the office to make that small investment, and it's something I regret. When she asked for one in our new home here in Pilaf, I took the time to do the opposite of what I did in the city. Instead of attending to an urgent need at the store, I asked Gracie to handle it as best as she could. Jennifer likes simplicity. Forget anything wireless and digital. She likes big and simple. I installed a round dial thermometer in a spot that was protected from the sun most of the time. It only took me thirty minutes to purchase and install. It cost me all of $8. You would have thought by the joy it brought my wife that the thermometer was a gold-plated, treasured heirloom. I'm glad that I had the chance to play that scene over again, and to do it the way it should have been done the first time.

Our Sunday morning group study was well attended today. Harry arrived early and drove in without incident. With great seriousness, he asked me where I was hiding the fig squares. Uh-oh. Was I supposed to make another batch? Then Harry broke out in a smile and grabbed one of the jelly doughnuts while he winked. Because Uncle Ben backed up a little to focus on an early chapter of Colossians, he took time today to look at the list of faithful believers at the end of the apostle Paul's letter. Imagine the honor of being listed in God's Holy Word as a faithful worker, using words like "standing firm," and "working hard."

Pastor O'Connor's message picked up where Uncle Ben's left off, encouraging all of us to stand firm and work hard with the right motive. I loved his quote, "A dark motive will ruin the kindest gesture." I know that truth all too well as someone who once offered what I thought was a kind gesture with a motive that was not perfectly pure. Come to think of it, I think I've received a few of these myself. I think most of us, to some degree, can relate to both sides of that equation.

Few worshippers left the church after the service ended. There was a lot of interest in the announcement that Donald Buckley wanted to share. When he started speaking, all the casual chatter instantly stopped. To everyone's delight, Buckley's Fruit Farm was sponsoring an apple pie baking contest open to anyone living in Pilaf. The specifics would be announced and posted on their web site in the coming days, but he did mention that this community event would take place on New Year's Eve at the church. There would be three judges. They apparently won't be from Pilaf. That makes sense. I wonder who they are? I have to assume it's nobody we know.

Looks like the mysterious vandal knows that Neil's cameras are rolling. The giant snow globe remains untouched. On one hand, I would have loved to see the instigator caught. On the other hand, I'm glad that law and order has returned to Minnetonka Street.

Monday, December 21, 2015, 8:39 a.m.

Monday is earning its reputation. The sky is completely obscured by fog and drizzle, the kind that will get you wet if you walk more than a block. I can barely make out the silhouette of the giant maple tree in the store's front yard. If I stare at it long enough, it looks like a creepy figure with its fingers curling toward me. That majestic tree doesn't deserve to be considered creepy, but getting that image out of my mind is a challenge. I'll wait for the fog and drizzle to clear so I can replace that image with one that honors its stateliness.

Both Mr. Rayburn and Miss Miller stopped in this morning. I think they walked in together, although I can't say that with absolute certainty. When Miss Miller was distracted in the the dry goods aisle, Mr. Rayburn hurried over to the counter where I was sipping my hot apple cider. He wondered if he could speak to me privately after school let out today. He was very specific about wanting to make sure it was in my office, and further still with the door closed. If I didn't know Mr. Rayburn as well as I did, I might have called Officer Caputo to conveniently drop by as school let out. He seemed to want to secure my agreement before Miss Miller emerged from somewhere in the aisles. Just as I agreed, Miss Miller reappeared with some baking ingredients.

After handing her the items in a bag, she handed it to Mr. Rayburn and asked if he could place it in her car. She did not want to fuss with it and risk having her hair get too wet in the drizzle. Mr. Rayburn was happy to help. The moment the front door closed behind Mr. Rayburn, Miss Miller quickly asked if she could stop by sometime to chat privately. I must have looked confused, because she immediately asked again as if I didn't hear her request the first time. The moment I agreed, Mr. Rayburn returned. Having been in big-city business for many years, I became quite savvy to what kinds of currents were really driving surface events, but this one has me totally stumped. I dare not share the odd exchange with anyone except Jennifer. Perhaps she can help shed some light on this.

I received a delightful email from Stormy this morning. He had a quiet moment in between his early and mid-morning weather feeds to send me a note of thanks for inviting him to play a small role in Harry's breakthrough. Small role? Without Stormy, Colossians 1:15 would not have been as clear as it became for Harry that day. He promised to come more than just once a year because he enjoyed the common bond that we all share, the Savior whose birth we celebrate. Stormy is a wonderful ambassador for Christ, a real class act.

Monday, December 21, 2015, 9:00 p.m.

If only I could somehow harness the energy that Joel and Jessie possess as we approach Christmas. Conservatively, I think they could power half of Pilaf. There is a half-day scheduled for tomorrow, but schoolwork is the last thing on anyone's mind, student or teacher.

As expected, Mr. Rayburn arrived at Bailey's front door around 2:15 p.m., when school let out for the day. He made his entrance with beads of drizzle glistening on his overcoat as the drizzle and dense fog persisted for much of the day. He wasted no time, motioning us to my office, and looking in every direction as though he was the most wanted fugitive in Ohio. His shoulders relaxed once the door was closed. What could be so important and so secretive that he would go to this extreme? He explained that both he and Miss Miller are apple pie aficionados and both were going to enter the big Pilaf apple pie baking contest on New Year's Eve. I quickly told him that I was not one of the judges, nor did I know any of the judges. Mr. Rayburn stopped me. He wasn't seeking favor. He was looking for some creative assistance in using the event to propose to Miss Miller, but was having trouble trying to chart a fun course that would lead to that end. I couldn't help smiling. I would not need to have a gentleman's pep talk with him after all. How could I not help? This event is going to end up eclipsing the pie contest! Mr. Rayburn pleaded with me to keep this a secret. Not even Jennifer should know. I agreed. I offered him a high-five before exiting the office, but he wanted to reserve the celebration only after Miss Miller responded to his proposal with a "yes." If you asked anyone else in Pilaf who knows the pair, it's a fait accompli. Now I wonder what Miss Miller wants? On this dreary Monday, it's appropriate to say that I haven't the foggiest idea.

Joel and Jessie asked if we could do a C.L.I.P. run every night this week until the day after Christmas. They want to know the exact day we hit 100. How could I resist? This is a chance to make wonderful memories that will last them both a lifetime. The counting was carefully and dutifully executed. We came home with no change. The "99" remains untouched tonight.

Tuesday, December 22, 2015, 10:10 a.m.

That brazen vandal knows no bounds. George just left the store fit to be tied. The globe was

nearly fully deflated only thirty minutes after he arrived at work, preparing for a heavy day of Christmas deliveries. The vandal left his or her mark in the same fashion as the other two times. The previous repairs were still intact, however George discovered another puncture, about four or five inches long, about a foot from the other two repaired punctures. This time, Neil's surveillance system was dutifully recording everything, at least George hoped it was. According to George, Neil almost took his system down on Monday assuming the vandal had been frightened away, but he became preoccupied with a decorating task with which his wife Dawn needed help. George called Neil and left him a voice message to let him know about the new breach. He asked me if I would contact Officer Caputo. Assuming Neil's cameras were recording, we may have our first solid lead.

Joel and Jessie were rising just as I left for the store. They were clearly excited that today's half-day at school would mean little, if any, actual school work. Since Jennifer needs to head to Giammalvo's Market for a few Christmas items this afternoon, she will ferry Joel and Jessie to the store to have lunch after school lets out at 11:45 a.m. They will stay with me here at the store this afternoon.

The sun has returned to Pilaf. The finely distributed moisture from yesterday's all-day drizzle froze overnight. It left a layer of what looked like a very thin coating of snow over everything. Once the sun came out, the delicate layer of frozen drizzle vanished from sight, at first only where the sun was shining. Eventually, it disappeared even from the shady spots. That would have made an interesting time lapse video. Perhaps someday I'll treat myself to one of those very small, all-weather video cameras to see the mystery of all that nature likes to keep secret.

Tuesday, December 22, 2015, 7:55 p.m.

According to Stormy Windham, the weather looks quiet through Christmas Day. We always look for that perfect snowfall to add the reflective glow to our Christmas lights, but a strong El Niño is keeping our December weather fairly mild and mostly tranquil. That's quite a contrast compared to the last couple of years. Stormy is speculating that there may be a stormy period shortly after Christmas Day. Pilaf won't really notice, I suspect, since people have taken an unusual interest in apples these days. It's not about baking apple pies for Christmas, either.

Miss Miller came into Bailey's in much the same way that Mr. Rayburn came in yesterday. Because of what I know, it was humorous. I had to be careful and wear my best poker-face, but even if I had not, Miss Miller looked so nervous that I don't think she would have given any thought to it, even if I had busted out laughing. I can understand Mr. Rayburn's nervousness, but I could not begin to imagine what Miss Miller needed to talk to me about until she pulled me over to the produce section. She confided in me that she was concerned that Mr. Rayburn would make a better apple pie than hers for the big New Year's Eve competition. She was concerned that if his pie was better than hers, that his romantic interest in her would fade. It took years for her to attract his attention and she did not want to blow it by making an apple pie that he did not like. She wanted to know what kind of apples that he bought for his pie so that she could adjust her recipe to make sure that he liked it. I tried to reassure her that everyone at the school talks exclusively about her apple pie, including Mr. Rayburn, and that she should stick to her tried, tested, and true recipe. I think I was able to convince her, but she still wanted me to pay attention to the ingredients that he purchased. I'm sure that Miss Miller thought I smiled to be friendly and reassuring, but I could hardly hold in my giddy, schoolboy laughter.

Neil stopped by the store just before closing today with all of the surveillance gear in tow. He would begin the task of analyzing all the video, looking for the daytime vandal who struck sometime this morning. Almost everyone is aware of the bizarre events on the steps of the Pilaf post office. We will all be glad to trade in this drama for the happier one unfolding on New Year's Eve.

Wednesday, December 23, 2015, 8:11 a.m.

Neil met George at the store as dawn barely showed signs of breaking along the horizon. He had his smart tablet with him as we all gathered around the counter with our mugs of coffee. George and I knew from Neil's body language that he caught the big fish. Neil prepared George for what he was about to see by telling him that he would have never guessed who the vandal turned out to be. Without having the video proof, not a single person would have believed an eye-witness account. With that, Neil played the video file.

Our eyes were fixed on the video of the giant snow globe as it played. Suddenly, the globe starts to deflate. Where was the vandal? George and I saw nothing! Neil stopped the video and played it again. George and I didn't understand why the globe started deflating. Was it simply a material failure? Neil replayed the video again and told us where to look as he zoomed into the lower right side where the two previous punctures were located. The vandal would have been easy to miss without zooming in. The vandal was not a "someone". It was a feathered some "thing." George and I both exclaimed in perfect sync: "Bonnie and Clyde!"

The fact that our fugitive is a black crow was not the end of the story. Neil told us to keep watching. There was no way of telling if this was Bonnie or Clyde. Where was the other crow? Moments later, a second crow arrived. That's when the first one made its way into the partially deflated snow globe while the other one appeared to stand watch. The one in the globe came out with the small hat that the snowman was wearing. It had a little trouble getting the hat out of the puncture slot, but eventually wiggled it out and flew away. The lookout took off seconds later. Bonnie and Clyde were truly earning their names in this town.

Locating the objects and preventing another break-in were next. George was going to call Officer Caputo to ask him to run up to Uncle Ben's place. Perhaps, like last year, they are stashing their goodies on his porch. Finding a way to prevent another puncture wound to the giant snow globe will be, in my opinion, the bigger challenge.

Wednesday, December 23, 2015, 4:30 p.m.

Pilaf is quiet. I love how everyone is quick to hustle home in the days leading up to Christmas. The most recent customer left the store more than twenty minutes ago. There is still plenty of road traffic driving past Bailey's, but everyone seems to have everything they need for Christmas Day now. Even Jimmy Giammalvo has mentioned that his food market seems to empty out more quickly in the mid-to-late afternoon hours. That's a good thing. It helps us to take a little more time to meditate on the magic of a love so great, that it motivated our Creator to devise a rescue plan that is irresistible to those of us being rescued.

Officer Caputo stopped by after the lunch crowd left. After hearing from George, he drove to Uncle Ben's, who had a hunch that a visit from Officer Caputo was coming. Apparently, the news about the snow globe traveled fast. It was mentioned as a late-morning side note during WPLF's crosstalk between the DJ and the news anchor. Now everyone is looking for a plastic candy cane, part of a plastic house chimney, and a miniature snowman's hat. Officer Caputo told me they both looked everywhere on Uncle Ben's property and found nothing. Even with all the radio press earlier today, there were no new leads.

We are now only a few hours away from Christmas Eve. I'm concerned that Joel and Jessie's C.L.I.P. number will remain stuck at 99. How could we get just one more house to put up something, even a few simple LED candles in the window? I'm not coming up with anything at the moment. I'm hoping for a little Pilaf Christmas magic between now and tomorrow night.

Thursday, Christmas Eve, 2015, 9:00 a.m.

I can't remember a Christmas Eve that looked and felt more like an early spring day. If it wasn't for the dark sky and very late sunrise at this time of year, you might have been able to convince me that I pulled a mini Rip Van Winkle and slept through Christmas and the roughest part of winter.

Who in their right mind would want to sleep through Christmas? Not even the Grinch.

Uncle Ben was in for a cherry Danish and coffee earlier this morning. He said he is continuing to look for the hot loot that his feathered friends stashed somewhere, but has had no luck. We have the weather helping this year since there is no snow to pile up and cover the missing items.

I also drove past the post office and saw that the giant snow globe was gone. I know full well that two crows cannot grab a deflated snow globe and fly away. My educated guess is that George took it back to his house to assess the damage. There's only so much duct tape you can use on an object before it starts to look dumpy. I'm sure I'll catch up with George at this evening's Christmas Eve candlelight service.

The kids did not even have to ask for their evening C.L.I.P. trip last night. After a wonderful family dinner, everyone chipped in and made clean-up a family affair. Once the kitchen was back in a state of order, I grabbed my jacket in front of Joel and Jessie and simply told them that I'd be waiting in the car. I didn't have to wait long.

Our drive, surrounded by majestic orchestral Christmas music, was full of anticipation. I drove nice and slow so that Joel and Jessie could count everything that they saw. After a careful tally, the C.L.I.P. number was still 99. I suggested that we do it again, and drive even more slowly. Getting no resistance, we retraced our path and started the drive from our home to Bailey's one more time. I stopped to point out what looked like a Christmas tree in a window across a field. Joel and Jessie reminded me that the decorations had to be on the streets we traveled, and not a house clearly on another street one block away. The second tally showed us all how careful the first one was. The number stands at 99.

The kids hid their disappointment well when we returned home, but I could tell that changing the number on the boards in their room would have made their night. There's always tonight.

Thursday, Christmas Eve, 2015, 3:19 p.m.

We had an unusually heavy Christmas Eve lunch rush today. It's always somewhat busy here at the store. The usual customers come in just to wish me a Merry Christmas and to sit for a moment and grab the complimentary eggnog and Christmas cookies that I always offer. There are other customers that swing by that I don't normally get to see very often because most of them are working when Bailey's is open. But because so many of them have Christmas Eve off, I have the privilege of catching up with their family news. Perhaps the lunch counter was a little extra busy because the word spread that Gracie made a couple of caramel-apple pies for dessert. If Gracie even thought about entering the competition, everyone else might throw in the towel spare a few, but she will be out of town for New Year's Eve.

Miss Miller and Mrs. Krumm sat together at the counter and ordered nothing but two slices of pie. I wonder if some of them came in just to get some ideas for the New Year's Eve apple pie baking contest? Donald Buckley has yet to update his website with all the rules. I imagine that will change by this weekend.

The lunch crowd came in like a Lake Erie snow squall, and left just as quickly. By 1:30 p.m., Bailey's was quiet. With everything under control and Gracie starting on a few of the pre-close items, I excused myself for a few minutes and went for a quick walk. The thought occurred to me that there was a house for sale a few blocks down from Bailey's and it was vacant. If I could contact the realtor, Adrienne Camp, I might be able to see if she would let me into the house to place a couple of LED candles in the window. It was at least worth a call. I took note of the number of the for-sale sign in front of the house and called. I left a message nearly two hours ago, but I haven't received a reply. Time is running out. I'd really like to help the kid's C.L.I.P. number round out at 100 tonight. Unless we have one hold-out that doesn't turn on their Christmas decorations until Christmas Eve, we may be stuck at 99. Pilaf isn't the kind of town that waits for Christmas Eve to express the Christmas spirit.

The moon has been getting big and bright this week. Despite no snow on the ground, the moon has added a nice ambience to the nighttime Christmas lights that adorn Pilaf. It was almost full last night. Stormy mentioned that the Christmas moon was going to be full this year. That doesn't happen very often. The next one after this year won't be until December 25, 2026.

Friday, Christmas Day, 2015, 6:59 a.m.

Merry Christmas! Sammy waltzed into the kitchen dragging a long piece of green tinsel attached to his hind leg. He must have been under the tree trying to get the tinsel to play back. As alluring as all of the ornaments, lights, and tinsel are, Sammy has largely been avoiding the tree this year. I'm not surprised given the tree's propensity to lunge at cats. Our trees have had a track record. The advantage, however, is obvious. Perhaps we will aim for better orchestrated, more deliberate replays in the years to come.

There's no place I'd rather be on Christmas Eve than in church with my family and friends. As much as I attempt to find the right words that describe the taste of heaven that reaches down and touches every single one of us, I cannot. There are no words powerful enough. Nothing captured the essence of our worship service more than seeing Harry Buser with a look of wonder and awe on his face that none of us had ever seen before. In fact, while singing Silent Night, Harry slowly raised his hands toward heaven. For someone who isn't known for being demonstrative, it was a special moment. Harry's expression started spilling over to others, especially the young people, as their hands began to rise. By the time we reached the last line, every hand was raised in the soft glow of Christmas lights in the sanctuary. Every single hand. That has never happened before. There were few dry eyes as we softly sang, "Sleep in heavenly peace."

Our evening meal after church was simple. A savory tuna casserole awaited us in the crock pot. We all continued to speak about sensing heaven touching our church service as we enjoyed our meal in the living room with a fire crackling in the fireplace. The fire was really more for ambience since the skies were brilliantly clear last night and the temperatures were cool, but not cold.

Before it became too late, I told Joel and Jessie that it was time for our nightly ride to count lights. I think I have been more excited about these nightly rides than they have. Perhaps it's because I know that decades from now, they will cherish the memory of their childhood Christmas moments. My only concern was falling short of 100.

We pulled away from the driveway admiring our own lights. Joel programmed chasing red and green lights on our roofline and it looked spectacular. Shouldn't we give our own house an extra point for creativity? Joel and Jessie reminded me that I knew "the rules." One point for the Rice home.

The near full moon cast a wonderful, bluish hue over everything. There were no other cars on the road, so I could drive as slowly as I desired, taking in the scene. Within a few blocks of Bailey's, Jessie cheered as she pointed out the passenger side window. It was a new Christmas display and it was spectacular! How could someone wait until Christmas Eve to throw the switch on something this nice? Then the shock hit me. It was the vacant house that was up for sale! How could anyone, even a team of people, decorate so fast? Could Adrienne have arranged this so quickly? Did I even give her enough information about what I had in mind for her to make this happen? I am still at a loss for words.

We returned home with two elated kids. The last thing they did before turning in was to erase the 99 on their boards and gleefully replace it with an even 100.

Soon, dawn will break. Controlled chaos will begin, but not before our traditional Christmas morning feast.

Friday, Christmas Day, 2015, 10:30 p.m.

Christmas music began filling the house, softly at first, when Jennifer and I first made our way to the kitchen at around 6:40 a.m. It has been going non-stop until just a few minutes ago. George would have been proud. There were very few songs that repeated more than once. Of course, that can't compare to George's collection, which is so large that he could go days without any Christmas songs repeating. I'll have to borrow a few more from his collection for next year.

How does Jennifer do it? Every gift that she wrapped had so much thought behind it. I was amazed when she passed me a rather large box. My curiosity was heightened when she told me that it probably wasn't a good idea if I shook it, something I have a tendency to do with gifts. With all eyes on me, I started to unwrap the gift. It was a wireless weather station, complete with every bell and whistle imaginable. How did she know that I had been thinking about installing one at Bailey's? Thinking it was too much of a luxury, I never shared my desire with anyone. When I asked her how she knew what to get, she did admit to having just a little assistance from a certain popular radio meteorologist. Amazing.

I wasn't sure if Joel and Jessie wanted to make an evening C.L.I.P. run, so I asked them how long they would be keeping track of the Christmas lights. They wanted to keep counting until the last Christmas display gets turned off and put away. Our evening drive was wonderful. Seeing the vacant house that is up for sale all decked out again was phenomenal. I must compliment and thank Adrienne when I see her. How she pulled that off I'll never truly understand.

Saturday, December 26, 2015, 7:22 a.m.

I'm sure glad Gracie is back. She opened the store today. I'll head in later this morning after I enjoy the afterglow of a memorable Christmas Day. I was tempted to say that it was a perfect Christmas Day, but that would then mean that all the others I've experienced were not perfect by default. Every single one of them has been perfect in their own unique way, so memorable is a better word.

Dawn is slowly breaking. It's another clear morning. I was up before Jennifer today and offered to make scones for breakfast. After a crazy few days in the kitchen, and a busy period coming with the apple pie contest ahead, she gratefully accepted the breathing room. I took orders for apricot, raspberry, blueberry, or apple-cinnamon last night. I was prepared to make them all, even if everyone wanted something different. Blueberry and raspberry won. They came out of the oven ten minutes ago. Since a fresh pot of coffee has just finished brewing, I poured a cup and I grabbed one of the blueberry scones while they were still warm. If this moment could be captured in literary terms, it is the period at the bottom of the exclamation point of a beautiful, mellifluous sentence.

I've been reading the setup instructions for the wireless weather station that I received from

Jennifer and the kids. I want to take full advantage
of Bailey's exposure to the atmosphere. To make
certain that I'm placing the sensors in the right
places, I plan to ask Neil Manausa for his help. His
flair with electronic gadgetry is second to none.
With the weather being so tranquil this December,
I'm hoping it will last a little longer, long enough to
see this unit telling me so much more than the
thermometer on Bailey's front porch. I thought
about putting it up here at the house, but Jennifer
and the kids insisted that I'd find it more useful and
fun to watch at the store. I think they're right.

Saturday, December 26, 2015, 4:55 p.m.

It was a busy day at the store today. Gracie
told me that it was that way from the start. I
wonder if the weather has something to do with it
since the day after a major holiday is usually pretty
quiet, especially Thanksgiving and Christmas.

Adrienne Camp took time to stop by the
store today since she was not able to return my
inquiry on Christmas Eve. I was anxious to talk with
her anyway. She was actually in a West Virginia

town whose valley was so surrounded by mountains that her cell provider had unreliable service. Instead of a call, she decided to stop by the store to see if she could answer questions about the property. Apparently, she did not understand my cryptic request. It suddenly occurred to me that Adrienne did not hear my voicemail until she drove out of that West Virginia valley on her way back to Ohio late last night. Then who decorated that house in such a festive way for Christmas?

After explaining to her what I wanted to do, Adrienne also wondered who decorated that house in the way I described. In fact, it was impossible since the power to the house had been turned off so that electricians could rewire some of the interior to bring it up to code. We both decided to walk over to the house.

We arrived at the front steps. I confirmed to her that this was the house that was lit up so majestically. There was no indication that there had been lights anywhere. Nothing on the porch or pillars. There were no lights around the windows. There were no electric candles in the windows. I told her that we all saw colored spotlights shining on the house. There were no spotlights anywhere. In fact, the house looked as barren as Adrienne expected it to look. She asked me if I was sure that the house we saw brilliantly lit was this one. Not only was I sure of it, but I had two other young witnesses who saw it before I did.

Since Adrienne had the keys to the front door, she opened it up and we walked inside. It was as barren as could be. There was evidence that the electricians were doing their work, but nothing that would even come close to suggesting that less than eighteen hours ago, there was a phenomenal Christmas display for all passers-by to enjoy. I felt like I was in an episode of the Twilight Zone. I know what I saw last night and it doesn't match what I saw this afternoon. We walked back to the store and tried to make sense of it all but we were both dumbfounded.

I'll make plans to drive our usual C.L.I.P. route tonight, but I won't say anything to the kids ahead of time.

Sunday, December 27, 2015, 6:54 a.m.

This year's Christmas afterglow has been a long and bright one. Virtually everyone's Christmas lights are still burning brightly 24/7, that is, except one house.

Joel and Jessie piled into the car with their pads and pens and waited for me after all the kitchen dinner dishes were put away. I wondered what we would see, particularly as we drove past the vacant house. Assuming it was dark, how would I explain that if they asked? I had no answer, and no plan.

The drive was a pleasant one. The near full moon was rising. With the temperature at 27°F, a thick frost was already visible, twinkling on the lawns and rooftops. It was thick enough to add a subtle reflective glow on many of the Christmas lights. I didn't think that the kids would notice, but they did. In fact, it was a bigger deal to them than I thought. They said that snow would be better, but that a "twinkly frost" was kind of special, too.

We drove past the vacant house not far from Bailey's, our official route's terminus. It was dark. There was no sign that there were any decorations anywhere on its frame. I was silent as we drove by, watching for Joel and Jessie's reaction, but there was none. Their joy was not diminished, nor did they even mention the stark difference in what we saw compared to Christmas Eve and Christmas Day. I must admit, I was tempted to ask them if they noticed, but why spoil the mood?

Unceremoniously, the C.L.I.P. number went down one notch tonight from 100 to 99.

Sunday, December 27, 2015, 4:55 p.m.

We enjoyed a phenomenal day at church, almost as though Christmas Day extended into this morning. There was a sense of anticipation as we all enjoyed a special hour of fellowship. With the conclusion of Uncle Ben's study on Colossians last week, we took this week to pray together as a group, then to enjoy a continental breakfast together.

The classroom windows were decorated with lights. Whoever decorated them took their time. It was meticulous work. In fact, it looked strikingly similar to the decorations that adorned the vacant house a few nights ago. After asking key people who would know about such things, not a single person knew who did such a great job with the room decorations. Even stranger still is that no one seemed to think too much about it. Perhaps I need to stop over-analyzing so many things.

While the pace of life here can't even compare to the crazy pace in the city, for Pilaf, the last few weeks have been hurried and hasty. I felt the need to consciously unplug after heading home from church. With Joel and Jessie playing with their cousins at Jim and Barb's house for the afternoon, and with Jennifer experimenting with her apple pie recipe, I thought that a walk down the Jasmine Creek foot trail may be just what I needed.

The sun was low, but bright. It shared the sky with a few decorative clouds. The wind was completely absent. One could not ask for a more picturesque December afternoon for a walk where my hiking shoes could collect a little dirt.

At first, I was thinking about every little thing that came into my mind. It was almost as though everything that happened in the last several weeks was crowding for center stage. I walked almost a half mile without even noticing the condition of the foot path, how fast the creek was flowing, or if any wildlife stirred around me. I had to purposefully reject any thought that tried to commandeer my mind. It took a few minutes, but eventually, I could hear the Jasmine Creek bubbling, even though it had been there for the last fifteen minutes.

Aside from the gently gurgling water and my breathing, there was near-total silence whenever I stood still. The sound of silence was beyond description. There's a spiritual dimension to this kind of hush. Perhaps that's what lies behind the Scripture passage in which God encourages us to be still, and to know that He is God. I've been too revved up and too plugged in to hear His sweet and irresistible voice.

There was some ice at the edge of the creek. I watched it for a while and began to marvel at the properties of water. It's the only known substance in creation that has its highest density as a cold liquid, and not as a solid. That's why ice floats. Most people don't even give this any thought since it's simply something that happens in nature. Every year, we see the ice begin to form along the shallow edges. It spreads and thickens after the New Year until it becomes thick enough to support our weight. It still amazes me that less than a foot of ice can support the weight of a car. Without this quirky phenomenon, life would not exist on earth. If ice formed on the bottom of lakes and oceans, the entire climate and ecosystem would be so different, that most conclude that life would not be possible at all. We sure do have a gracious and amazing Creator to make cold water more dense than solid ice.

Monday, December 28, 2015, 9:00 a.m.

Something about Stormy's voice caught my attention and made me listen. He sounded more serious than usual as he spoke about an impending storm during his morning weather segment. This apparently would not be the kind of storm that would cripple the area with snow as we experienced last December. The offending element would be a sustained period of strong winds. There would be some rain to start and perhaps a little snow at the end of this windy system, but the wind may cause some issues by Wednesday.

I looked at the weather station that Jennifer and the kids gave me for Christmas and thought the looming storm would give it a proper baptism. George has a very tall extension ladder that he uses to decorate his house for Christmas. I'll leave him a message to ask if I could borrow it for a day to mount the wind portion of the weather station on Bailey's roof. I'll need a few materials to do that. A trip to the hardware store is in order once the morning chores are done.

Details, rules, and entry forms for the highly anticipated apple pie contest have been posted on Buckley's Fruit Farm's web site. Judging from the hit counter on the bottom of the page, the judges will have quite a few pies to taste. Donald has not yet released the names of the three judges, but we now know that all three judges are from out of town. Furthermore, to insure that the playing field is level in every way, the pies will be assigned an entry number. During the contest, only Donald will know whose number belongs to which baker, so the entire Buckley clan will not be eligible to participate.

There was a fun twist added to the contest, a twist that will help with Mr. Rayburn's plan. Each contestant must bake two identical pies, one of them to be sampled by the judges, and one whole pie to be auctioned off for the church missionary fund. The second whole pie is what Mr. Rayburn and I will focus on to execute his proposal to Miss Miller. I'll schedule a quiet meeting with Mr. Rayburn this afternoon.

Monday, December 28, 2015, 5:34 p.m.

George stopped by during his deliveries this afternoon. He received my message and it stirred his curiosity since I did not tell him why I needed his telescopic ladder. He was more than happy to lend it to me, but he wondered what I needed to reach.

After all, anyone who wanted to put up Christmas
lights finished that task weeks ago. I was able to
show him my wireless weather station. The best
place for the wind measuring cluster was obviously
going to be as high up as I could reach. That would
be the peak of Bailey's. The only object that was
taller was the giant maple tree about a hundred feet
west of the store. The distance from the store alone
would prevent it from being a wind shelter. George
said that he would bring it over and place it on the
west side of Bailey's tonight so that I could work on
my project in the morning. He assumed that I
wanted to get it up and operating before the windy
system blew in later this week. He must have heard
Stormy's forecast for Pilaf.

Mr. Rayburn was next in the sequence of
people to stroll in. Not only was he there to grab
some apples, but it was the perfect time to craft a
plan of action for his big night. Since he was not yet
aware of the rules of the contest, I brought him into
the office, closed the door, and called up Buckley's
web site. At first, he thought the second whole pie
put up for auction would complicate things, but I told
him that it was the best set-up he could have hoped
for. The first pie that the judges would taste would
be the decoy. The engagement ring would be placed
in the middle of the auction pie, but covered by a
small piece of pie crust in the middle, making a small
dome. I would make sure that Miss Miller would win
that pie since the baker of the pie can write a note in

advance that gets delivered with the pie. The note will be Mr. Rayburn's proposal.

Mr. Rayburn loved the plan, but wondered how I could make sure that Miss Miller was the highest bidder on his pie? I didn't dare explain to him what I already knew about Miss Miller's desire to attract his attention and hold it. I told him that he would have to trust me. Then he showed me the ring. I nearly fell back from its size and beauty. Mr. Rayburn has good taste. I told him to start filling out the online forms while I checked on the apple supply.

I'm glad that I closed the door behind me. I ran into Miss Miller by the apples. She asked me if she could see me in my office. I did everything that I could to convince her that now was not a good time. My stall tactic wasn't working. She worked her way to my office door when her phone chimed. She pulled her phone from her purse to read a text. I have no idea what that text said, but suddenly she had to leave, but would return later. I can't remember that last time my heart raced that fast from anxiety.

Mr. Rayburn had no idea that Miss Miller was seconds away from discovering him and a beautiful engagement ring in my office. He was too engrossed in signing up for the contest. There was no need to tell him.

Tuesday, December 29, 2015, 10:49 a.m.

Neil Manausa made time for me this morning. He arrived at 8:15 a.m. I bought him a muffin and a cup of coffee. We had the chance to chat a little before we went to work installing the anemometer. Neil said his wife Dawn was busy preparing to make her apple pie for the contest. The field of contestants is filling up. I hope the judges, whoever they are, bring a very big appetite.

George did as he promised. I checked the side of the store even before unlocking the front door. The ladder was exactly where he said it would be. George purchased it about six years ago when he decided to add Christmas lights to the very peak of his roof. Since then, he was able to add a variety of articles that he would not have otherwise been able to place. A good example was last year's wireless speakers that are mounted on both of his neighbor's homes. George won't need the ladder returned until later in January when he reluctantly removes and repacks his decorations until next November.

After Neil's last swig of coffee, he rubbed his hands indicating that he was ready to mount the anemometer. To avoid any last-minute run to the hardware store, I picked up some of the mounting brackets I thought we would need last night. Neil said that it was important to make sure that the cluster was perfectly level to insure accurate samples. He brought his digital level to make certain. Because there are no wires to run, the only other task was to make sure that the selected location had a decent amount of sunlight since a solar panel keeps the unit's transmitter battery charged. No issue there since Bailey's peak is the highest point within a hundred feet. Once Neil loosely secured the anemometer to Bailey's peak, he asked me to walk around to make sure I was happy with its position. Once I gave the okay, he tightened all of the screws and bolts. He chuckled and said that the only way that would come down in a storm is if Bailey's found itself spinning aimlessly inside a tornado headed for Oz.

Before Neil came down from the roof, he asked if I had left any kind of decorations near the chimney. It looked like a collection of items that were forgotten and stuffed in a corner along with some twigs and rags. Having never decorated Bailey's roofline, I could not imagine what Neil was seeing. He climbed up on the roof and walked over to the chimney, collected the items under his arm and slowly made his way back to the ground. Once we spread the items out on the ground, a great mystery was solved. Amongst the sticks and rags, there was a plastic candy cane, a deflated plastic chimney, and a snowman's hat, items that Bonnie and Clyde had systematically removed in the last several weeks. I would have never guessed they wanted to build a nest on Bailey's roof. I had seen them from time to time near the store, but the pair of crows have been virtually everywhere in Pilaf at some point in the last month or two.

The collection is cleaned off the roof and George's somewhat mangled items are in the back of the store. If George doesn't stop by today, I'll call him to let him know that I was able to reclaim his items out of Bonnie and Clyde's pawn shop.

Tuesday, December 29, 2015, 4:26 p.m.

Just as Stormy predicted, the winds are picking up. This time, I can do more than casually estimate the wind. My new weather station began to faithfully wire back its data to the console this morning. The winds are now gusting to 22 miles per hour. I'll have to email Stormy some of my observations if he finds them helpful. The automatic data uplink was not set up yet, so I would not have access to my new weather station's data from home tonight. Neil said he would return soon to help me set that up. Isn't technology grand?

Miss Miller returned early this afternoon. She did not seem as anxious to speak with me as she was yesterday. Instead, she spent time looking over my dwindling apple supply. Eventually, she asked me if I had any Braeburn apples. I thought I had a few, but when I checked, I saw that they were gone. I offered to call Giammalvo's Market to see if they had any. As I walked to my office, I motioned to Miss Miller to follow me and to shut the door. I would call Jimmy in a moment.

Framing my question in the desire to help her get Mr. Rayburn's attention, I asked her if she would be interested in knowing what pie was his so that she could make sure that she won the auction on his pie. She asked how I could be sure since the pies are only going to be numbered. I asked her to trust me. After making certain that I was not kidding, a grin ran across her lips. She agreed.

Since decorations on the pie table were fine, I showed her a bright red candle shaped like an apple. I would make certain that this candle would be sitting right in front of Mr. Rayburn's pie. My instruction to her was simple. Make certain that her bid is the highest one for that pie. She could not contain her excitement. The idea of making a fuss over Mr. Rayburn's apple pie was as romantic as an apple pie contest could be. I then picked up the phone to call Jimmy Giammalvo, but Miss Miller told me she would drive down to Giammalvo's Market to check for the Braeburns herself.

Wednesday, December 30, 2015, 9:05 a.m.

Spooky. I can't describe it any other way. Given the fact that we have a contest that the whole town has been talking about, and we are only a few days away from ushering in a brand new calendar year, Pilaf shouldn't look like a ghost town.

Stormy was right on the mark. Last night's wind was hard to ignore. The sound of the wind actually woke all of us at various times during the night. When it was time to wake up, the house was dark and the power was out. Only a few emergency lights in a couple of our outlets were illuminated. Since the house was still warm, I assume the power went out not long before I got up to start my day. I was able to start a cozy fire in the woodstove so that everyone would stay warm. The winds are definitely colder compared to when we retired for the night.

There was virtually no traffic on the road during my drive to the store. I saw several large branches down along the way, but no major damage. I had hoped to see lights on in some of the homes, but there were none. The strangest thing was seeing Pilaf go from a brightly lit Christmas town last night to a barely visible series of dark, steel-gray silhouettes. Bailey's was just as quiet and dark as everyone else's place. No power. It was cool, but not cold in the store. Like our home, the cool was no match for the woodstove once the fire got going.

My new weather station certainly did receive quite a baptism. The console recorded a peak wind gust of 53 miles-per-hour at 5:03 a.m. That's about when the power was knocked out. The gusts continue, but they have held under 40 miles-per-hour since arriving a couple of hours ago.

The implications of this power outage suddenly hit me. How will Pilaf bake its apple pies today? Most people were waiting for today to bake them. I know of only one person who was planning to make their entry yesterday, and that was Maureen Whittles. Is it possible that she will win the contest by default? More importantly, how will the impact of a long-lasting power outage change Mr. Rayburn's plans for tomorrow night? This is not good.

Wednesday, December 30, 2015, 9:29 p.m.

Not long after writing this morning's entry, the power thankfully returned. For the first hour, the lights flickered. Each time they did, I held my breath and prayed. By late-morning, life in Pilaf started returning to normal. Customers arrived, many of them scrambling to pick over the last of the dwindling apple supply. I suspect that many of those who looked panicked at the low supply were bakers who decided to enter the New Year's Eve contest at the last moment.

Both Mr. Rayburn and Miss Miller arrived only minutes apart for lunch. I saw them chatting for a few minutes before sitting at the counter and deciding to have lunch. I asked Gracie to wait on them since I did not want to inadvertently slip in speech, especially since I was trying to walk gingerly on two sides of the same fence. She told me that both had a bowl of tomato bisque and a slice of pie, blueberry pie. I suppose we are all going to be eating our fill of apple pie beginning tomorrow evening.

Donald Buckley stopped by. George and Uncle Ben were at the counter when he arrived. He looked mighty relieved that the power had been restored to the entire town by noon. Unfortunately, the storm that blew through caused numerous delays and cancellations at Hopkins Airport. Not until Donald elaborated did I draw the connection to tomorrow's big event. Part of the judging team was flying in and their flight was affected. Donald was heading north to meet them at the airport when they called to say that they were stuck in Boston. They were trying their best to rebook a flight to Cleveland but were running into barrier after barrier and wondered if we knew anyone who could help.

Fortunately, Uncle Ben has a friend who works as a flight dispatcher for a major airline. After a few quick calls, he put Donald in touch with Pete Schenck in Minneapolis. Fifteen minutes later, Donald received a text from the judges once stuck in Beantown. They were being shuttled to another concourse and placed on a direct flight to Cleveland. Is there anything else that we don't know about Uncle Ben's connections? Probably. He never ceases to amaze us. I'm still wondering who these judges are and where they are coming from? Donald isn't talking.

It's still somewhat windy this evening, but nowhere near the powerful gusts that panicked Pilafians with a power outage earlier today. In the final hour at Bailey's, no gust was higher than 25 miles-per-hour. The temperature on my new console and the porch thermometer were both reading 29°F. I'm enjoying my new weather station.

Joel, Jessie, and I just returned from our evening C.L.I.P. ride. Anyone that knows Pilaf could have predicted what would be on their boards tonight. That's right, 99. It may be Groundhog Day or later before we see the C.L.I.P. dwindle to zero. This has been an interesting exercise. I do wonder if the kids will bring it back next year.

Thursday, December 31, 2015, 6:00 a.m.

I love quiet mornings like this. A powdered-doughnut coating of snow was waiting for my gaze out the window this morning, but at least the wind is completely gone. A power outage is something that Pilaf would rather do without. Jennifer's window thermometer reads 19°F. I could have guessed that without looking. There was a slight chill near the sliding glass door.

Jennifer's two Mount Mansfield pies look mighty tempting. They are painstakingly covered and protected from curious furry four-foots, and inquisitive two-foots as well. They sure look like winners to me. Surely the mystery judges will see it my way. Regardless of the outcome, Miss Miller will declare Mr. Rayburn as the clear winner tonight, even though everyone from her school declares that nobody can rival Miss Miller's apple pie. It's one of the most anticipated New Year's Eves in Pilaf that I can ever remember.

Sammy strolled into the kitchen when he heard that I was up. He looked at Jennifer's pies, then looked at me as if he was insulted that they were covered so securely with two large, glass cake covers. As if I understood his body language, I shrugged my shoulders. He seemed satisfied with that.

I'm planning to close the store early today. With so much energy being focused on the contest tonight, things will become quiet immediately after the lunch crowd exits. Gracie is off today, so I'm anxious to clean up quickly, close the store, and get settled at the contest before the crowd arrives. I want to make sure that apple candle is sitting next to the correct pie.

Thursday, December 31, 2015, 2:55 p.m.

My forecast was as accurate as most of Stormy's. No sooner did the lunch crowd thin out, the only traffic I saw after 2 o'clock was Mr. Rayburn. He showed me his pie and it was truly one-of-a-kind. The little dome made of crust at the top was on both pies, but only one of them had the engagement ring. The other one had a stemmed maraschino cherry inside the crusty dome. While I could not tell the difference between the two, he made absolutely certain that he could distinguish between them. After reassuring him that I would be there early and place the apple candle in the right spot, he sauntered out with a whimsical spring in his step. I recognized the gait. I'm sure it was the same one that I had only hours before I proposed to Jennifer.

Bailey's door has been locked for almost thirty minutes now. Clean up was quick. Time to round up the family and head to the church hall. Let the fun begin!

Friday, January 1, 2016, 9:16 a.m.

If the way in which 2015 ended is any
indication of how the new year will play out, this is
surely going to be a memorable year in Pilaf. For
starters, and as expected, there will be a wedding
sometime this year! Mr. Rayburn's carefully crafted
plan, however, did not unfold the way it was
envisioned. That's what made the last few hours of
2015 so memorable. Some might say that my
previous sentence is a gross understatement.

The church hall was beautifully decorated
for the contest. Macintosh red and Granny Smith
green LED lights framed every pie table. There were
even giant, inflatable apples placed throughout the
hall. My guess that George donated them was
correct. After locating Mr. Rayburn's unmistakable
pie, I positioned the apple-shaped candle in front of
it. The number assigned to his pie was #16. I also
recognized Jennifer's Mount Mansfield pie. Hers
was labeled with #22. All-in-all, there were twenty-
five entries. The three out-of-town judges would
have their hands (and stomachs) full.

The church hall was packed, but well-
organized. I recognized most everyone, but there
must have been others from out-of-town attending
thanks to all the radio publicity. After everyone
enjoyed a sloppy-Joe dinner, Donald Buckley took

center stage with a microphone and offered a wonderful welcome that made every pie baker feel like a winner.

Everyone wanted to meet the mystery judges. Donald managed to keep this a very tight-lipped secret until it was time for the judges to become the focus of everyone's attention. He called them in one at a time. The brief introduction to Judge #1 led us to believe that virtually everyone in Pilaf has heard of his name. Surely that was not an overstatement when he called out everyone's favorite radio meteorologist, Stormy Windham. What a delightful choice!

Donald then told us that Judge #2 and #3 actually came together as a pair. We immediately thought a husband-wife team, but he stumped everyone when he stated that this completely impartial pair lives in a town very similar to Pilaf. The town was not Borger, Congress, Seville, or Burbank. The distance that this couple traveled to be present was over 3,500 miles. The whole room began to murmur in disbelief. Was Donald kidding? We all saw how serious he was when he introduced Mr. & Mrs. Craig and Anne Linaker, all the way from Fleetwood, United Kingdom! Everyone cheered when they walked in as though they were the Beatles. Donald and Jimmy Giammalvo worked on flying them in for this grand event. Jimmy knows that the pair love American-style apple pies. They apparently did not hesitate to accept the invitation.

So this was the pair who was stuck in Boston, and almost did not make the event.

The judges were released to their work of sampling the twenty-five pies while everyone else was given the word to visit the tables and to place written bids on the pies. Separately, both Mr. Rayburn and Miss Miller strolled by where I was seated, each giving me a nod. They both looked so calm, cool, and collected, while my heart raced knowing what was about to transpire.

Some time later, but before midnight, the judges had made their decision. Everyone took their seats and became quiet. Donald took center stage once more to announce winners of the contest. He took out the white ribbon and announce that the third place pie went to my bride, Jennifer Rice! Jennifer beamed with the applause. The biggest surprise was when the red, second place ribbon was given to Mrs. Sauerkraut's apple pie! Everyone in town knew that she made some of the best pecan pie around, but nobody knew that her apple pie was just as delicious. The crowd was perfectly still when Donald held up the blue ribbon. After a long pause, Donald announced the winner as Miss Miller! The crowd erupted in instant applause. Everyone at the school knew that she would probably win this contest, but now it's official. Mr. Rayburn was pleased for her and gave her a long hug.

Next, it was time to award the auctioned pies. All went well until Donald announced that pie

#14 went to the highest bidder, Miss Miller. I thought there must be some mistake. Panic struck me when I did a visual check of the table. The apple-shaped candle was not at pie #16. Miss Miller grabbed pie #14 and the note that went with it while I tried to find out who moved the candle. The Andersons saw my panic and came over since pie #14 was Amy Anderson's pie. I asked them if anyone knew how the apple-shaped candle migrated over two pie positions. That's when Amy's husband Rick chimed in. He said that he saw their four-year-old daughter, little Annie Anderson, wandered over to admire the candle earlier in the evening. After picking it up, she wandered down a few pies and placed it back on the table, but in front of the wrong pie. It was their intention to return the candle back to where it was, but there was so much going on that they simply forgot.

I ran over to Miss Miller who was just reading her note. It was clear that she was confused. How is it that she bought Amy Anderson's pie, and not Mr. Rayburns? I explained to her what happened. By the time we returned to the auction table, they were auctioning pie #18! Who was the highest bidder on Mr. Rayburn's pie, #16? Rick Anderson said that a gentleman that he never saw before won the pie. He picked up his pie and the proposal note and went out the door. There were only initials on the sheet. The top bidder was simply listed as "J.R."

Mr. Rayburn came running to me. Miss Miller, who was angry that she had bought Amy Anderson's pie, was standing next to me. After explaining what happened, and realizing that I probably ruined the night for the both of them, Mr. Rayburn got on one knee, took Miss Miller's hand, and proposed. Miss Miller was so shocked that she dropped Amy's pie on the floor while screaming her "yes" for the whole church hall to hear. Mr. Rayburn was embarrassed that the beautiful engagement ring and a written proposal had found its way out the door with a complete stranger. The more he tried to explain where the engagement ring might be, the harder Miss Miller giggled. He didn't know which emotion to express until Miss Miller started laughing hysterically and with reckless abandon. No one had ever heard Miss Miller laugh like that before. Soon, everyone, including Mr. Rayburn, was laughing because Miss Miller's laughter was so contagious. Even with the comedy of errors, the world was all right once again as the clock struck midnight.

Several questions remain though. Who is J.R., and where is the the engagement pie? Right now, no one has a clue.

Special thanks:

To some real people who allowed me to weave them into this work of fiction. Certain people and places may be real, but the situations in which I placed them are all fictional, a product only of my crazy, unbridled imagination. You know who you are! (All other persons are fictional characters. Any resemblance to anyone real, living or dead, is completely and totally coincidental, fluky, random, and serendipitous.)

Adam and Kate Vodicka, who posed for the book cover along with the phenomenal apple pie supplied by my mother-in-law Pat Schmies. My father-in-law Howard Schmies, better known as the "Geauga County Genius," sacrificially offered his taste buds to make certain that the apple pie was better than Miss Miller's.

Editor Dawn Manausa, whose eagle-eyes focused on making sure all of the content made sense, and that Mrs. Krumm would give this book an "A" for grammar, spelling, and punctuation; (<---Ooops. I think you finally missed one, Dawn.)

Made in the USA
Columbia, SC
02 September 2017